Why do their paths keep crossing?

"My name is Kyle Trent. I'm an attorney, live in Harrisburg, Pennsylvania; marital status. . .unattached." He waved his arm toward her, indicating it was her turn.

"I'm Hester Lawson, journalist, live in Detroit."

He regarded her, his eyebrows raised in a questioning manner.

"Unattached, too," she admitted reluctantly.

"When I first saw you, I was returning from a business appointment in Pittsburgh. A week before that, my plans had already been made to come here and check some wills and deeds. I'm not following you; my business is perfectly legitimate. What is your reason for being here?"

Hester hesitated, not wanting him to know how long she would be in the region, but she finally said, "I'm on assignment now in the town of Afterglow."

He laughed delightedly. "Really! I have some business interests in Afterglow, too, and if you see me there, don't entertain the wrong idea. I planned this trip weeks ago."

"A likely story," she said.

IRENE B. BRAND is an award-winning inspirational romance novelist who has written numerous novels and articles. A retired teacher, Irene resides in West Virginia when she is not pursuing her other active pastime—international travel.

Books by Irene B. Brand

HEARTSONG PRESENTS
HP9—Heartstrings

Afterglow

Irene B. Brand

Heartsong Presents

A note from the author:
*I love to hear from my readers! You may write to me at
the following address:* **Irene B. Brand
Author Relations
P.O. Box 719
Uhrichsville, OH 44683**

ISBN 1-57748-070-8

AFTERGLOW

Cover illustration by Randy Hamlin.

PRINTED IN THE U.S.A.

one

"But I've never compiled a history," Hester Lawson protested to her friend, Belle Noffsinger, who had telephoned to warn Hester that she would soon receive an invitation from Mayor Arthur Stepp to write a history of the town of Afterglow.

"There's a first time for everything," Belle laughingly said, echoing the homespun philosophy of the Appalachian region where she lived. "Besides, you're a journalist," Belle argued. "Writing a history shouldn't be so much different from your newspaper work. Our mayor is determined to hire a professional writer for the job so Clint and I recommended you, and we do hope you'll consider it."

"I wouldn't have much to write, would I? Haven't you always said that you live in a town where nothing ever happens?"

"It's quiet now but Afterglow had its moments in the past."

"I don't know," Hester said slowly. "I would love to see you and now that Mother is dead I intend to travel some, but I hardly had a little Appalachian town in mind. How many people live there. . .five hundred ten?"

"Oh, it's five hundred eleven now," Belle retorted. "We had a birth yesterday. Seriously, I don't want you to feel obligated but I know you can do it, and I thought you might as well have the ten thousand dollars as anyone else."

Hester whistled. "Where did a little town get so much money?" she asked in her low, husky voice.

"I thought that would get your attention," Belle said with a laugh. "Clint wrote a grant proposal to fund the project. Of course that money has to pay for the printing of the books, too, but you should receive half of it."

"Thanks for telephoning in advance; it will give me time to consider. I do need a change of pace. I've been busy with Mother's care for so long and now I find myself at loose ends."

"Don't you have any other relatives?"

"A few cousins and an aunt on my father's side, none of whom live in Detroit."

Talking to Belle brought back pleasant memories. They had been roommates in college and had kept in touch since then. Because of Hester's busy schedule, she seldom wrote letters, though she did telephone Belle occasionally. But Belle wrote often, long narratives describing her life in Afterglow, the town where she had gone to live with her newspaper husband five years ago. She had described Afterglow and its residents in such detail that if Hester did take the job, she would probably recognize many of the people she saw on the street.

Hester hung up the phone, feeling more at peace than she had since her mother had become ill. She heard Molly, rattling pans in the kitchen, and she headed that way, a wide smile lighting her face.

Molly turned from the sink where she was preparing a salad. "It's great to see you smiling again. Must have had good news."

"Not particularly, but my friend, Belle, phoned. It always picks me up to hear from her. She wants me to come to their town to do some work."

Hester reached for a cookie and Molly smacked her hand. "Stop that. You'll ruin your dinner and I've got your favorite, roast beef, tonight."

Hester popped the whole cookie into her mouth and laughed at Molly's frown, wondering what she would have done without this woman over the past five years. About the time Hester's mom, Anna Lawson, had become ill, Molly's husband had died and she had moved into the house to help Hester. She had been there ever since.

Hester inhaled the aroma of the roast beef surrounded by carrots and potatoes as Molly set the platter on the table. It was not difficult to pray a blessing over this food.

"Thank you, God, for our food and for this kind woman who has helped me through my trouble. What would I have done without her or You during my mother's illness?" Hester prayed with tears pricking her eyelids.

Molly patted her on the back. "You're the daughter I never had, Hester. You've helped me more than I've helped you." After they had filled their plates, Molly said, "But about going to see your friend, that's a great idea. And if I can give you some more advice, why don't you sell this large house? You shouldn't live here alone. There are too many memories."

"You can always live with me," Hester said in surprise. She had supposed that Molly would continue to stay with her.

"I've been thinking of going to Florida to visit my sister. She lives in a retirement home and she wants me to join her. At least I want to go down and check it out."

Without Molly being there, Hester wondered how she could possibly have enough courage to come home every evening to an empty house.

"I know I need to make a change. I talked to my boss today and asked him to reassign me to a job that would require some travel."

For several years Hester had been the assistant editor at a local newspaper, which kept her in the office most of the time, and, understanding her depression, the editor had agreed. But God would also understand her need for a change of pace and she wondered if this call from Belle was the opportunity she sought.

"Do you believe in coincidences, Molly?"

"Maybe, but I believe more in faith in God and that He daily provides for us. If it's right for you to take that job your friend suggests, you'll know it without a shadow of a doubt." Molly pointed to a framed sampler hanging above the table.

In All Thy Ways Acknowledge Him
And He Shall Direct Thy Paths
Proverbs 3:6

Hester had embroidered the sampler as a child and her
mother had framed it. For years she had trusted that promise
as a guide for her daily living.

But at thirty years old, single and proud of it, was she too set
in her ways to start a new life? Although her mental attitudes
might hinder a change to another job, her physical traits would
not be a detriment. She had glowing, gray eyes that took on a
green hue when she became angry. She was of medium height
with a supple body enhanced by a slow, graceful walk. She had
worn her brown hair short for years to accommodate her busy
lifestyle, and most people classed Hester as beautiful. But in
her opinion, the slightly long, straight nose inherited from her
mother did not compliment the delicate bone structure of her
face.

Hester stretched lazily and Molly said, "Want a dish of ice
cream?"

"Not just now. I'm trying to settle Mother's estate and I
stopped at the bank today and brought home a packet of documents from the safety deposit box. If you don't need help
with the dishes, I'll look through them."

"Won't take me long to put everything in the dishwasher.
Do your work but take a little time to relax. I'll be in my room
if you need me."

Hester walked into the comfortable living room, cozy in its
simplicity. There were deep chairs, an afghan-covered couch,
an entertainment center with bookshelves holding a television
set and a CD player, floor lamps conveniently located beside
the comfortable chairs, and a coffee table holding several
magazines, Hester's Bible, and a recently published devotional
book.

Although usually not one to procrastinate, Hester had been

slow to settle her mother's affairs, for once that was done, the loss would seem irrevocable. Anna Lawson had died the first week of December and Hester had taken only her mother's will and insurance policies from the bank and had waited until after Christmas to look at these other things. The holiday had been a hard one for her but she had struggled through it with Molly's help and by accepting the hospitality of her church friends. Since Hester was the only heir, there hadn't seemed to be any need for hurry. She put a disc in the player and turned the volume low and the soothing piano music of Dino flowed around the room. She kicked off her shoes and spread the contents of the file folder on the coffee table.

The file contained income tax returns dating back ten years, some certificates of deposit jointly held by Hester and her mother, her parents' wedding certificate, their birth records, as well as her own. Finding nothing that needed any immediate attention, Hester laid aside all of the documents except her parents' wedding certificate. She had not seen it before and she considered framing it to hang beside the portrait of her parents made ten years ago, before John Lawson's death.

Hester admired the colorful wedding certificate bordered with delicate garlands of roses and apple blossoms, but she gasped when she noted the date on the document. Quickly, with shaking fingers, she retrieved her birth certificate from the file. Still not certain her eyes were not deceiving her, she went into her mother's bedroom and looked at the family Bible's record. There was no doubt about it. The date on the wedding certificate was one year later than the one in the Bible. The day and month were the same, but the year in the family record was different and indicated that her parents had not been married until one month before her birth.

Hester sank weakly on the side of her mother's bed. *Why hadn't my parents told me?* There had never been any doubt that her parents were happily married, so why had they waited so long to wed when they knew she was on the way? It was hard for Hester to accept the fact that her parents had not been perfect, but the evidence in front of her was too strong.

Hester replaced the wedding certificate in the file and the next day during her lunch hour, she returned the documents to the bank. She no longer wanted to have the certificate framed.

Before Hester left the newspaper office for the day, her supervisor called her into his office. "I've been checking into a new line of work for you. We could possibly use you occasionally in the sports department to travel with the university's women teams and report on their activities. At first it would be in this country, but you might eventually make it overseas."

"I'm rusty on who's who in sports now because I haven't kept up with that information for the past few years; however, I'm sure I could pick it up quickly. When you decide, I'd like to consider it." She laughed slightly. "I had another job offer last night. I've been asked to write the history of an Appalachian town by the name of Afterglow. Ever hear of it?"

The editor shook his head.

"I wouldn't have heard of it, either, except that my college friend, Belle, moved there when she married. They would give me several thousand dollars to compile the book, but that would still be a cut in my income because it would take six months or more. I'm not sure I can afford that."

"Sounds like it might be a welcome change for you. All of your friends here have been concerned about your health. Working full-time and then being on vigil in your mother's bedroom each night has drained you. The atmosphere of a small town might be good therapy for you and you could probably send us human interest stories from the area. We could keep you on the payroll as a freelancer and pay you for the articles you submit."

"I'm not much interested in it, though, so keep the sport's job open for a few days."

"Looks like the letter came from that man," Molly said when Hester came home a half hour later and entered the kitchen. "I put it on the table in the living room. Take this cup of tea and relax while I finish dinner."

Before Hester opened the letter she recalled how Belle had described their town official. "Mayor Arthur Stepp is a short man with a barrel face and a rotund stomach, who walks as if he has bunions on both feet. . .and he probably has."

Hester read the message thoughtfully. The mayor's letter extolled the virtues of his town. Afterglow had been founded one hundred years ago as a railroad center for the timber industry. The city council had voted to commemorate the town's origin with a six-month-long celebration scheduled to start in May and culminate with a grand-slam weekend in October. The history would need to be finished before October, therefore work on the book should be started as soon as possible.

When Molly came in to announce dinner, she said, "Any more interested now than you were before?"

"I don't think so." Hester rolled off the couch and went to the bookshelves and took down an atlas. Turning some pages, she said, "Here it is. Looks as if Afterglow is located in a small river valley nestled among two high ranges of the eastern Allegheny Mountains."

Quickly checking the mileage, she continued, "It's about six hundred miles away and three hundred miles farther south of us, so if I do go I could avoid our Detroit winter."

"If it's in the mountains, I doubt it will be summerlike," said Molly.

For the rest of the evening, Hester pondered the situation. From her correspondence with Belle, she had deduced that nothing much ever happened in Afterglow and no doubt the town's history would be dull. When she weighed several months of living in Afterglow with the excitement of following women's sports events, there really wasn't much choice. She hated to disappoint Belle, but tomorrow night she would write Mayor Stepp and decline his offer.

The next day, however, brought a development that not only reversed Hester's immediate plans, but set in motion a series of events that marked a complete change in her future.

When Hester arrived home, one lone envelope, a communication from the United States Postal Department, lay in her mailbox. The brief statement indicated that a bag of mail, lost for thirty years, had recently been recovered and that every effort had been made to forward the missives to the intended recipients or, lacking that, to their next of kin.

With a laugh, Hester said aloud, "I doubt anyone would have written to me that long ago." But amazed, Hester lifted a tattered envelope addressed to her mother at her childhood home in Kentucky, which was strange in itself since her mother was a child when she had moved from that town. Who would have known to send a letter there? The name on the envelope was her mother's maiden name, Anna Taylor. Another word had been written after Taylor but it had been erased, indicating the sender may have written "Lawson" and then had obliterated it.

Though her mother was dead, Hester still hesitated about opening her correspondence, but she was curious. Using a letter opener, she slit the yellowed envelope and quickly scanned the contents, then read it a second time, her heartbeat accelerating with each word she read.

> *Anna,*
>
> *I couldn't believe that you were gone when I returned from my tour of duty in Korea. Your last letter mentioned the baby. Why did you run away? You know I would have taken care of you. Since I don't know where you are, I hope your relatives will forward the letter. You know where I live and I beg you to contact me. I love you, but I'll not push*

myself on you. You must make the next move.

T O BY

What did this mean? Who was Toby? What baby? Hester's mind churned maddeningly, relating this letter with what she had learned just last night from her parents' wedding certificate. Did it indicate that this Toby was her father rather than John Lawson? Hester rejected the idea. John Lawson was all that anyone could have desired in a father. Of course, he was her father. And where had this letter been for thirty years?

Hester carefully examined the envelope and small sheet of paper for a clue as to the sender, but there was no return address and the postmark on the envelope was smudged so much that she could not identify it. She made out a few letters, *Af gl w* and then using a magnifying glass, she spelled the word, *Afterglow.* Laughter was Hester's first reaction, for it was inconceivable that she would receive two unrelated letters from this obscure town within two days. Of course, there might be hundreds of towns by that name, but after scanning the atlas for a half hour, she had not found another Afterglow. Hearing Molly entering the kitchen, Hester hastily concealed the letter. This was one thing she could not share with anyone. Surely there was some mistake!

But the coincidence was more than Hester could dismiss from her mind and she spent a fretful night. Should she meddle in her mother's past? She might be better off not to know who had sent the letter and why. But she could not ignore the matter. She brightened a little when she thought the addressee might be another Anna Taylor rather than her mother, but she had to renounce that supposition because her mother really had lived in that Kentucky town for several years and Anna's grandparents had made their home there until their deaths. No, the letter was to her mother and so it concerned Hester. Could she go to Afterglow with the twofold purpose of writing the history of the town and surreptitiously searching out the mysterious Toby?

The next day, Hester moved sluggishly around the office, earning her many curious glances from her fellow workers. Finally, unable to bear the indecision, she wrote a brief note to Mayor Arthur Stepp.

> *I'd be pleased to accept your invitation to compile a history of Afterglow. Expect me in your town in about fifteen days.*

She dropped the letter in the outgoing mail and stopped by the editor's office to tell him of her decision.

"I'll give you a year's leave of absence, if it takes that long, but still keep you on the payroll for freelance work," he assured her. "You'll probably find some great human interest stories. I understand some of those mountainous areas are fifteen to twenty years behind the times."

Once the decision was made, Hester did not fret about it, especially since Molly was enthusiastic about her plans. Molly put her bony arms around Hester. "It's for the best. I'll go to my sister's in Florida for a few months and when you return to Detroit, I'll come to you if you need me, but I'm sure you'll be adjusted by then."

"Plan to live with me when you've had enough visiting."

"I want you to find a good man and get married, Hester, and if you do, I'll not be living here."

Hester laughed away her suggestion. She had hoped Molly would stay in the house, but so quickly did she find a church family who wanted to rent a place to live for six months, that she considered it was another reason to believe that God was guiding her decision.

When she telephoned Belle that she was coming, her friend said, "Great! You can live with us."

"I won't, although you're sweet to offer. No friendship can withstand months of live-in company. I'll roost with you for a few nights until I can find some accommodations. Is there a motel?"

"Of sorts, but you wouldn't like it."

"A hotel?" Hester asked hopefully.

"Yes, but it closed about twenty years ago. I suppose you could stay at Miss Eliza's. Her grandmother started a boarding-house here at the turn of the century when the timber industry was strong, and Miss Eliza has carried on the family tradition. She keeps a few permanent boarders. It's not too bad."

"Oh, yes, I remember about Miss Eliza. You mentioned that she travels around town like a runaway train, and that her face turns a ruddy red when she's angry."

"Your memory is too good. I hope you won't repeat any of the things I've written about our townspeople and make them angry with me. You'll be here only a few months, but this is my home."

"Trust me. I'll be discreet. But about lodging, try to find a place for me."

"Telephone the night before you'll arrive and I'll give you directions."

"Remember I grew up in Detroit? If I can drive in our congested traffic, I should be able to find my way around Afterglow."

"Oh, you won't get lost once you arrive. It's finding the place that will pose a problem. You'd better telephone me."

❧

Hester kept packing items in her compact car until she could not see out the rear window and knew she would have to rely on the side mirrors. Probably she was taking too much, but she would be away during the winter and summer, so that required all her clothing, and she would also have to take her computer. She bought a year's supply of paper and other office supplies for she figured the shopping selection in Afterglow would be meager.

As she packed, Molly kept warning. "You can't put all of

that in the car, Hester. Pack lightly as I've done."

Molly had packed her clothing in one suitcase and a shoulder bag, believing she would have more than enough garments to last her through the winter.

But Hester did not pay much attention. Emotionally, she still could not give up her mother and the home they had shared, and she had to take some family reminders with her. Even if she had only one room in Afterglow, she wanted it to remind her of home. She wrapped several of her favorite wall hangings, but with the automobile full of necessities, she knew she would have to leave the paintings behind. She replaced all of them on the walls except two. She had to take the oil entitled, *Winter Serenity*. The rural scene had been painted by one of her professors, I. M. Thomas. A distinguishing feature of his work was that he included the figure of a bird in each of his paintings. In this work the artist had depicted a long, narrow river valley wedged between a series of mountain ranges; the tiny figure of a cardinal perched on a snow-laden spruce in the foreground.

Thomas had been an artist-in-residence one winter at Ohio State University where Hester had been a student, and she had attended two of his seminars. She recognized that she did not have any great talent, as did Thomas, but he seemed content to let her dabble. Thomas had painted *Winter Serenity* to illustrate the use of oils, and when names had been drawn for the works he had painted, Hester had won the winter landscape. Since that time she had kept it above her desk for inspiration and she would not consider going to Afterglow without it. She took a sweater from one of her suitcases and replaced it with the painting. She tucked the sampler bearing her motto, "In all thy ways acknowledge Him and He shall direct thy paths," in beside the landscape, and her packing was finished.

Two days later, Hester saw Molly on a plane headed for Florida and, with a tingle of anticipation, she headed out of town. She had planned two days for travel to Afterglow in case she should run into slick highways, and the weather cooperated at first, but it started snowing at Pittsburgh and she crawled for miles on Interstate 79. She stopped around dusk at a motel north of Fairmont, West Virginia, fearing to travel any longer. Accustomed to lots of snow, she had no trouble coping with the wet highway, but another concern caused tremors of fear along her spine. *Am I being stalked?*

She had first become aware of the man on Interstate 80 as she traveled across Ohio. He had smiled at her as they passed in a service area. The next time she entered a rest stop, he pulled in behind her as she started to leave. He smiled again, but this time she ignored him. His dark blue Mercedes was not hard to spot and, keeping a careful watch in the side mirrors, she noted that his car kept the same distance behind her. When she accelerated, his car speeded up. When she stopped for gas in Pittsburgh, he pulled in at a pump behind her. Thoroughly angry and somewhat frightened, she drove on without filling her tank. Driving faster than she should have on the snow-covered road, she had left the man behind her and she breathed easier when she did not see him again. She kept watch on her gas gauge and was thankful she had enough fuel to take her to a motel.

Fortunately, there was a restaurant adjacent to the motel, for by the time she registered and paid for the room, the snow was several inches deep and, after bringing her bags into her room, she crossed the driveway to the restaurant. The warm food revived her spirits and she laughed at herself for thinking the man had been following her for he did not look like a stalker. Dressed in a dark business suit, the handsome man was of unusual height with a trim stature and his brilliant blue eyes were both beautiful and friendly. Most women would have been pleased to have a man like that pursue them, for he was handsome enough, but she had reported too many stories about women traveling alone, being assaulted.

The next morning, before she got out of bed, Hester flipped on the television and the local forecaster announced that the snow had stopped at midnight and that road crews were busily clearing the highways. She bounced out of bed, eager to be on her way. She pulled aside the curtain and peered out the window and her joy in the day dimmed—parked beside her loaded vehicle was the blue Mercedes that had followed her yesterday.

two

Thoroughly frightened and without even taking time for a shower, Hester hurried into her garments and picked up her overnight bag. She opened the door and peered intently up and down the parking area. No one else seemed to be around. She pitched the door key onto the dresser, closed the door quietly, and ran to her car. She shoved some accumulated snow off the windshield and unlocked the door.

"Dear God, let this car start now." She turned the key and the engine hummed into action as if it had spent the night in the insulated garage at Detroit instead of in this windswept motel lot. She breathed easier when she pulled out onto the highway and the Mercedes had not moved. Hester drove twenty miles before breakfasting, and after she had eaten and telephoned Belle of her whereabouts and the Mercedes and its attractive driver had not appeared, her tense nerves relaxed. No doubt she would never see the man again but it annoyed her that she was still harassed by the memory of his sparkling blue eyes; shiny white teeth; firm, straight mouth; and magnetic persona.

As she steered her compact Ford up the curving hollow, following the twists and turns of the river, Hester appreciated the wisdom of Belle's insistence that she telephone for directions. Many unmarked roads led off from the narrow paved highway, and if she hadn't had Belle's instructions, "Don't leave the main road. Afterglow is at the head of the hollow. When you get here, you can't go any farther," she would have gone astray more than once.

A few miles before she reached the town, the river veered to the left and her heavily loaded car slowly navigated a tortuous road up the side of a mountain. At the crest, she pulled into a lookout area for a bird's-eye view of the town of Afterglow. Although a few hemlock and spruce trees dotted the hillsides, deciduous trees, now barren of leaves, dominated the forest. Snow flurries danced in the air, but Hester left the car to peer over the precipice, jumping back in alarm when she saw the sheer drop below her. Thankfully there was a waist-high retaining wall! A sharp blast of wind swept up the hollow, so she hurried to the car and made her descent to where the river had reappeared hugging one side of the narrow valley.

She stopped abruptly when she came to a wooden, covered bridge spanning the river at a narrow spot. Although the huge timbers and beams that made up the frame looked sturdy, she wondered if it was intended for automobile traffic. She glanced up and down the river and could see no other place to cross. While she hesitated, a pickup whizzed across the structure, so Hester warily steered her car up the incline and bumped along the uneven floorboards, emerged on the other side, and crossed a rumbling, seemingly abandoned railroad track. The buildings of Afterglow spread up the valley as far as she could see until a curve in the river cut off the view. Dwellings perched in neat rows partway up the mountainside.

Why, I've seen this valley before! Since she knew she hadn't, Belle's description of the valley must have been more vivid than she had imagined.

"I'll meet you at the *Courier* office," Belle had said. "It's on Main Street and easily found. You might have trouble finding our house until you grow accustomed to the narrow, steep streets."

There was only one stoplight in the town and according to Belle, after passing the light, the *Courier* was on the right-hand side of the street next to the river. Hester saw the stoplight several blocks downstream as soon as she drove out of the covered bridge, but before she came to the light, she had to maneuver around a statue in the middle of the street. Hester had a brief glimpse of the inscription: CIVIL WAR VETERAN.

Before Hester had the car parked, Belle was on the sidewalk to greet her. Hester fondly appraised her friend's slanted blue eyes, fair complexion, and tawny hair, noting with amusement that Belle was more chubby than she used to be.

Hester was soon enveloped in Belle's arms. "I was beginning to worry. You're later than I'd expected you to be."

"I'm not used to these crooked roads and then, too, I stopped a few times to gaze at the fantastic scenery. No wonder you like it here."

"Wait until you see the trees with their leaves on. It's more beautiful then. Come in and meet my family."

Tall, angular, slow-spoken Clint Noffsinger was a native of Afterglow and he had met Belle when they both had worked in Washington, D.C. He greeted Hester with a warm handshake.

"And here's Ina," Belle said, lifting her three-year-old daughter from behind a chair where she had been peering timorously at Hester. "She's not normally so bashful, as you'll soon find out. You can see she's the spittin' image of her daddy, as the locals describe it." Belle looked fondly at her brown-haired, dark-eyed offspring.

"How was your trip?" Clint drawled. "Anything exciting happen on the way down?"

Although Hester had thought she would relish telling her friends about the encounter with the suspected stalker, she seemed reluctant to mention it. *Is it a memory I want to cherish for myself?* Strange how many times she had thought of that man today.

"I encountered about fifty miles of snow-covered roads yesterday. That wasn't exciting, but it was nerve-wracking."

Belle zipped Ina into a one-piece hooded suit. "We'll go home and have dinner ready when you finish work, Clint." To Hester, she said, "The centennial commission meets tonight, and the mayor wants you to attend."

Hester moved her purse and road maps from the front seat to make room for Belle and Ina in the car. She followed Belle's directions and turned left at the next street, but Hester gasped as she looked—straight up!

"How do you ever drive off that hill when there's a snow?"

"We don't; we walk."

Hester gunned the engine and her loaded car labored up the incline. "Walking wouldn't be much better," she muttered.

"We don't have many snows down in this valley. There can be a foot of snow on the mountain and we'll have only a smattering. Our home is the last one on this street. You can park behind the house."

"Whew!" Hester breathed deeply when she turned into the driveway and switched off the engine.

"Bring in all your things," Belle said. "I'll help as soon as I take Ina inside."

Hester shook her head. "I have everything I'll need for a couple of days in these two small bags, and I don't intend to stay here longer than that." When Belle started to protest, Hester glanced at the bungalow. "Now, Belle, be realistic. You have only four rooms and I'm going to be here for months. I'll need working space and privacy. I'll be in and out often and I won't stay in your house all of the time."

With a sigh, Belle agreed. "I suppose you're right, but I feel so cut off from the outside world, and I would enjoy some stimulating conversation. About the most exciting thing that's happened in the past month was when old Mr. Byrd dropped his false teeth in the soup kettle at the boardinghouse."

"I'll try to liven things up," Hester promised. "And with that comment on the boardinghouse, I don't think I want to live there."

"Oh, Miss Eliza was on the alert and she dumped the soup. You don't have to worry about her food. She's an excellent cook."

At dinner, when they discussed a place for Hester to stay, Clint suggested, "Why not try for the furnished apartment Miss Eliza has? Her nephew lived there at one time and she refurbished it a few years ago for a schoolteacher who moved to Afterglow. It hasn't been rented since the teacher retired and left the county. It may not be what you're used to, but you won't do much better on rental property in Afterglow."

"How many rooms?"

"Three, I think. Miss Eliza will be at the meeting. We can ask her about it," Clint said.

❧

Hester rode to the town hall with Clint, who was on the centennial commission. She eagerly looked forward to seeing the people she would work with on this project. Clint parked along Main Street and opened the door for her to enter a building two doors north of his newspaper office.

"We're meeting in the council chamber," he explained. When they entered the room, most of the chairs at the oval table were already occupied. A rotund man standing at the head of the table sped in their direction and extended a pudgy hand toward Hester.

"I'm Mayor Arthur Stepp," he stated. "Welcome to Afterglow."

Hester considered herself of only medium height yet she looked down on Mayor Stepp, who resembled a compact barrel. What he lacked in size, though, he made up for in action for his body appeared to be in perpetual motion.

"Sit beside me," he said, pulling Hester along by the hand. "I'll introduce you to the commission."

As soon as Hester settled into the chair, he said, "Starting to your left is the pastor of the Brown Memorial Church, Ray Stanford." When Stanford started to rise, the mayor said,

"Not necessary to stand on formalities, Reverend."

The mayor talked so fast his words ran together and she could hardly understand him, making it difficult to put names and faces together. She did note that the only other female in the room was Eliza Byrd, a woman who appeared to be in her early seventies but straight as a ramrod and with snappy, big brown eyes. Deep wrinkles encircled Miss Eliza's large mouth and her long, thin gray hair was braided around her head.

When the mayor had finished the introductions, he said, "Miss Lawson, we appreciate that you've taken time to help us celebrate the centennial of the fabulous town of Afterglow. By writing our glorious history, you will help us honor our ancestors who settled this rugged valley and brought the benefits of civilization to kith and kin."

The mayor rambled on in this vein for another five minutes, often interspersing his words with a hearty laugh and animated gestures, causing Hester to wonder if he could talk without waving his arms.

Clint Noffsinger sat directly across from Hester and he lowered his left eyelid slightly, suggesting to her that not all of the town's citizens shared Stepp's exalted views. But Hester was hardly prepared for Miss Eliza's interruption.

"Oh, hush, Mayor. Let's get on with the business of the evening. Miss Lawson will soon learn enough about our town."

Hester smothered a gasp at this rudeness. The mayor's face flushed and he threw an indignant glance in the speaker's direction, but he cleared his throat and forced a laugh.

"No need to be so hasty, Miss Eliza."

"There is a need for hurry," she retorted. "With all of the highfalutin ideas you've come up with, we should have started on this project five years ago. We don't have any time to spare. Let's fill Miss Lawson in on what we want her to do so she can start."

"I'd prefer all of you to call me Hester," she said. "From Mayor Stepp's letter, I assumed that my only assignment is to research and prepare a history of the town for publication."

Mayor Stepp cleared his throat again. "And incidentals connected with it."

Ray Stanford's bass voice sounded at her side. "We've planned a drama in October to feature highlights of our heritage. Perhaps you can find time to write that as you research the history."

"I suppose I could," Hester said slowly, "although I've never written a drama."

"And to direct it, too," Clint said with a grin. "The commission wants to be sure you earn your money."

"This promises to be an interesting year," Hester replied wryly. "May I hear about the rest of your plans?"

"Miss Eliza is looking for descendants of the first settlers to bring them in for our celebration," the mayor said.

"Hester," the old woman said crisply, "this town was founded by Hezekiah Brown, who started timbering here a hundred years ago. He had enough influence to bring in the railroad, which came up the valley and over the mountain to haul his product to market. Out of his vast holdings, he gave the land for this town. It's his memory we will be honoring."

Mayor Stepp motioned to the large man at her side. "Pastor Stanford will chair a committee to emphasize the coming of the Gospel to our community. Would you tell Miss Hester what you're planning?"

A massive man in his midforties, Ray Stanford resembled a lumberjack more than a preacher. His frizzy black whiskers bristled with vitality.

"The first Christian witness here was a chapel car ministry. Soon after the first train arrived, a missionary couple, Ivan and Thelma Hartwell, came into the community in a specially built car that contained their living quarters and a chapel. They pulled the car off onto a siding and stayed in the community for the better part of a year until they had organized the nucleus of our church."

"And according to my grandfather, they had a rough time of it, too," Miss Eliza said. "The wood hicks weren't pleased to have preaching in the town."

"Wood hicks?" Hester asked.

"The Appalachian word for lumberjack," Clint explained.

"Pastor Hartwell," Miss Eliza continued, "braved the saloons with a gun in one hand and a Bible in the other before he finally gathered a congregation."

"At any rate," Ray Stanford said, "we've made arrangements to have a passenger car converted into an exact replica of the one the Hartwells used and it will remain in the town as a permanent display. It will be delivered during centennial week."

"I've wondered how the town received its unusual name," Hester said.

Bewilderment covered the faces of those around her as they looked from one to the other. Mayor Stepp stammered and cleared his throat a few times, and finally Clint said, "I guess no one has ever tried to figure that out, Hester. Maybe you can find that out for us, too."

Hester did not bat an eyelash, but by now she was convinced that she was going to earn every penny she made in Afterglow.

"And we're planning other events throughout the year," the mayor continued. "Belle Noffsinger is in charge of a big craft show in July. We're going to refurbish the covered bridge, which is almost as old as the town, and we'll reenact a bank robbery by the Benson gang."

A man across the table from Hester said, "There's still a mystery about that robbery. Lots of people at the time thought that Benson stashed the gold somewhere. The law was hot on his trail and the heavy gold was delaying him. Haven't you heard that, Miss Eliza?"

"Yes, but I think it's quite unlikely that he left the gold behind when he fled. Besides, my grandfather said that for twenty years after the robbery, there was somebody combing these mountains for the gold cache and it was never found."

Mayor Stepp fidgeted during this exchange and he said, "Let's not stray from the subject, please." Turning to Hester, he smiled widely. "It's going to be an exciting year. You'll be glad to be a part of it."

"Don't forget the log raft expedition in May," Clint said. "That's the way logs were transported before the railroad arrived," he explained.

"What we need now is a lot of publicity," the mayor said. "Clint, you'll have to give the centennial plans more coverage."

"I'll do what I can, but the *Courier* doesn't have a wide circulation."

"Would you like for me to run articles in my Detroit newspaper?" Hester asked.

"That would be a great idea, young lady," the mayor said. "We need all the publicity possible."

"I wonder how much leeway I'm going to have in writing this history. As a journalist I've been taught to publish the truth. How will the residents react if I uncover uncomplimentary information about the town?"

"I'm sure you'll not find anything derogatory about our citizens, but by all means, publish the truth. You have a free hand," the mayor assured her with a sweep of his arm.

"Any suggestions about where I should start?"

"There are boxes of old papers on the second floor of the *Courier*," Clint said, "left there by the former owners. I've never looked at them, but they should contain much pertinent information."

"You should check the records at the county seat, and we have several cabinets full of old church minutes," Ray Stanford offered. "You would no doubt find those helpful."

After the meeting adjourned, Clint made his way toward Miss Eliza, who had already taken her coat from the rack and was buttoning the fur collar around her neck. He motioned for Hester to join him.

"Miss Eliza, Hester wants to find a place to stay while she's here. Would your apartment be available?"

"Certainly. But it's been vacant a long time. I would need some time to have it cleaned."

"Belle will bring Hester down tomorrow morning to look at it and see if it's adequate for her needs."

As they drove home, Clint said, "The mayor gets carried away, but he means well. He's in his midfifties and although he wasn't born here, he's become a regular Chamber of Commerce all by himself. He thinks Afterglow is a Garden of Eden, but we natives know plenty of flaws in our history."

"How's the mayor going to react if I do turn up some seamy stories?"

"He'll be determined that you won't publish them, that's what."

"And I'll be just as determined that I will. Perhaps I should have a written agreement with the mayor before proceeding any further."

"It's advisable."

❧

The next morning, Belle and Hester drove through town with Belle pointing out landmarks and Ina chattering from her car seat behind them.

"The old hotel is on the left, two blocks west of the *Courier*. When it was built about seventy-five years ago, the springs flowing from the mountainside supposedly produced mineral water. That didn't prove to be true, but the hotel enjoyed some success until the timber industry petered out about the time World War II started."

"What about coal mining?"

"There isn't much coal on this side of the mountains. A few mines were opened up in the county, but their supply of coal was meager. This area is in an economic slump, for progress has bypassed us. Without a through road, the tourists haven't found Afterglow. Rumors have it, however, that the old

Brown acreage around the town is being considered for a state park. If that happens, Afterglow's success would be assured, for it would be the only town within the boundaries of the park, which should make it prosperous again. Mayor Stepp believes this centennial celebration will bring tourists to Afterglow, who will return often if the park becomes a reality."

Belle stopped her car in front of the Byrd boardinghouse, a Victorian dwelling located on the south end of town, and Miss Eliza stepped out on the porch to greet them.

"My grandfather built this house around the turn of the century," Miss Eliza explained as she ushered them through a hallway overcrowded with heavy oak furniture popular a century ago, and into the large room facing the street. The living room furniture was also Victorian, but newly upholstered, so that the room was inviting and comfortable.

"He started the furniture factory," Miss Eliza added as she invited her guests to be seated.

"Oh, is there a factory?"

Eliza shook her head. "Not anymore. Ownership passed from our family many years ago and the last owner couldn't make enough money to keep it open."

"Do you have any information on the factory that should be included in the history?"

"I have several things in the attic. And you can interview my father. He's ninety-five and still alert."

Oh, yes. . .the man with the loose false teeth.

After she contributed more information about the town's history, Miss Eliza directed them through the wide hall and out onto the back porch. She indicated a small house a few yards away.

"There it is," she said. "It was originally built by my grandfather as a stable for his horses. He was like Mayor Stepp, always thinking on a large scale. Even though he never owned more than one horse at a time, he built a stable large enough for a cavalry herd. In my youth, we used it for vegetable storage, but my nephew remodeled it into an apartment."

"I'd like to look inside."

"It's open. Help yourself."

Miss Eliza reached out her arms to take Ina, then Hester and Belle crossed the small backyard to explore the building.

"I was in this apartment a few years ago," Belle said as she opened the door.

A shivery sensation possessed Hester when she stepped into the room. Of course, the building was unheated, but it seemed that more than cold had caused the shiver. . .almost as if she were stepping back into time. *Is this centennial research getting to me?*

"There hasn't been any heat in here for years, I'm sure," Belle said, sniffing. "It will be difficult to remove the musty smell from everything."

"Except for that, it isn't so bad," Hester said as she examined the tiny kitchen with an apartment-size stove and refrigerator, a table, two chairs, and overhead and base cabinets surrounding the two-bowl sink.

"I've considered leaving my home for smaller quarters," Hester said with a laugh, "so this should make me happy, but I won't have room to entertain a great deal."

A bed, nightstand, and a dresser crowded the bedroom, but because of its sparse furnishings—a couch, one chair, and two end tables—the living room seemed large. A garishly colored linoleum covered the floor in all the rooms.

"I'll need a desk, but otherwise, this will do quite well for temporary housing."

Surveying the sparsely furnished room, Belle said, "There's plenty of space to move in a desk."

Hester shivered and pulled her coat closer to her body. "Wonder how the place is heated?"

Belle pointed to a grill on the living room floor. "There's a gas furnace underneath this room. Only one register, but it should be enough for this small space."

"Probably I should take it," Hester said, "since you think it's the best quarters available." For some reason, she was reluctant to rent this house, but she had to have a place to live.

Belle must have sensed Hester's hesitation, for she said, "There are other apartments for rent but this one is the most convenient."

Before making her decision, Hester asked Miss Eliza about the cost of renting.

"Nothing at all, my dear. You're doing our town a favor to come here and write this history. You pay the utility bills and we'll call it a deal. Give me a couple of days to have the place cleaned and heated, and you can move in."

With that done, Belle and Ina returned home after leaving Hester at the entrance to city hall. She entered the mayor's office at his invitation and hearty welcome.

"And what can I do for you today, Miss Hester?" he said after he ushered her to a comfortable chair in front of his tidy desk.

"Before I start working, shouldn't we have a contract citing my responsibilities as well as the obligations of the town?"

Stepp waved away the suggestion with a languid movement of his hand. "Is that necessary? A gentleman's agreement is all we usually need in Afterglow."

"But *I'm* not a gentleman and I prefer to have a contract."

"By all means then," he hastened to please. "You write out what you think is necessary. I'll have my secretary type it and we can both sign the agreement. It won't require much time to take care of the matter."

Hester considered it preposterous that she be asked to write her own terms, but she took the yellow pad he pushed toward her. She found it difficult to concentrate on the content while the mayor expostulated on the glory of Afterglow and its heritage, but after several erasures and additions, she produced a simple document.

> *This agreement is made between the centennial commission of the town of Afterglow and Hester Lawson. Hester Lawson agrees to research and compile a history of the town of Afterglow to be ready for printing within six months of this date, and also to write a centennial drama and direct its production during the month of October.*
>
> *For her services, Hester Lawson will be paid approximately six thousand dollars, depending upon the cost of printing the book. If Lawson fails to meet the deadlines mentioned in this document, the centennial commission will be under no financial obligation for the unfinished work.*
>
> *The commission also agrees that Miss Lawson will not be restricted in the publication of the true facts that she uncovers in her research.*

Hester handed the rough copy to Mayor Stepp. "I know we hadn't discussed my rate of pay, but I understood that I was to be given the amount of the grant not used for printing. Clint says that the printing costs shouldn't exceed four thousand dollars."

The mayor scanned the agreement, smiled approval, and hustled into his secretary's office. Two copies of the document were soon duly dated and signed and Hester returned to the Noffsingers' home with her copy.

That night, Clint looked over the agreement. "Looks legal enough to me." Then with a laugh, he cautioned, "But don't underestimate the mayor. He's been known to wiggle out of a bargain if he's displeased with the results."

three

Hester awakened at four o'clock, her usual hour for arising in Detroit so she would be at the office in time to complete work on the early edition. Accustomed to the morning sounds of a city awakening—the delivery trucks, the garbage workers, the street sweepers—the quietness of this mountain village seemed even more thunderous than a city's clamor. After twisting and turning in the bed for an hour, she heard a rooster announcing the break of day and she decided that if it was time for him to be up, she could at least turn on the light.

The frigid room discouraged getting out of bed, so she propped two pillows behind her back and reached for a notebook on the nightstand. She studied the notes that she had made the night before, wondering if she hadn't been presumptuous in agreeing to this assignment and probably foolish to have agreed to be paid only if she completed the history on time. How could she possibly research one hundred years of Afterglow's history from an unreliable source of data, shape her findings into a manuscript suitable for a history, write a drama, and produce it in less than nine months' time? It could not be done. And how could she go about unraveling the mysterious letter addressed to her mother? It had all seemed so simple when she was in Detroit, but now she did not know in which direction to turn.

By the time she heard Clint and Belle stirring and noticed the smell of heat as the furnace warmed her room, she muttered, "I wish I'd never heard of Afterglow." But she had heard of it and now she had to deal with the assignment she had accepted. Yet, knowing what she had to do did not make it any easier. The room seemed like a prison until Belle tapped on the door to say that Hester could take her turn in the bathroom.

After breakfast, Hester and the Noffsingers lingered over cups of coffee.

"You don't seem to be rested this morning," Belle said with concern. "Are you one of those persons who can't sleep unless you're in your own bed?"

"Usually I can sleep anywhere. But I may as well admit it: I'm terrified of what's before me and I don't even know how to start."

"Why don't you start by taking a tour of the town?" Belle suggested. "Become acquainted with our fair city."

"That won't take long," Clint said with his one-sided grin. "Afterglow is laid out along the widest part of the river valley. You'll find most of the business district, both past and present, along the one main street and a few of the businesses are on the side streets. The residential area is mainly spread out on the mountainside. Do you want a guide?"

"No, I got my bearings when Belle drove me around yesterday, so I'll explore on my own." But remembering her recent experience on the highway, she added, "That is, if it's safe enough."

The Noffsingers seemed not to understand until Hester said, "You know what I mean. . .what about muggers or stalkers?"

Clint and Belle laughed simultaneously, and Belle said, "Have you forgotten you're in Afterglow. . .the place where nothing happens? The last crime we had in this town was when Mayor Stepp's housekeeper took him for a burglar, hit him over the head with a skillet, and he was admitted to the hospital with a concussion. We don't even lock our doors at night."

Hester grinned wryly. "Remember I'm from the big city. How would I know?"

A wail from the bedroom indicated that Ina had awakened,

and when Belle went to look after her, Hester said to Clint, "Do you know anyone in Afterglow by the name of Toby?"

Clint thought a moment. "No, I don't believe so. In the newspaper office, I come across the names of about everyone in town. Is this someone who lives here now or in the past?"

Hester kept her eyes focused on the coffee mug she held in her hands. "I don't really know. He's probably a man in his fifties. I'm not sure that he ever lived here. I wonder if there are other towns named Afterglow?"

"I wouldn't be surprised, but I don't know of any."

Hester had considered telling Clint and Belle about the Toby letter but decided not to because it seemed to cast a shadow on her mother's character.

"Oh, well, it's of no matter anyway." She looked out the window, where the sun had finally peered over the mountain to shed a brilliant light around the Noffsinger home. "How cold is it? Do I need to bundle up?"

Belle entered with Ina in her arms and handed the child to Clint. She looked at the indoor/outdoor thermometer on the wall. "It's thirty-five degrees now and there's a stiff breeze."

"I had the television on for the early news and the weatherman said the temperature will reach the midfifties today," Clint added.

"Then I'll dress as I would for a brisk walk in Detroit."

After she helped Belle with the dishes, Hester put on a hooded parka over her sweats and donned heavy socks and fleece-lined boots. A pair of mittens completed her garb. Since it was ten o'clock by then, she said to Belle, "Don't expect me back for lunch. I'll find a snack downtown."

"Have fun. Dinner at six o'clock."

When Hester stepped out onto the sidewalk, a blast of cold mountain air swept over her and she breathed deeply. But her lungs were not used to such fresh air and she coughed lustily before she resumed her normal breathing pattern.

A downhill walk soon brought her to Main Street where she

turned left. Many buildings had empty storefronts, but she saw several restaurants, a department store, a couple of bars, some grocery stores, a pharmacy, and even a video shop, post office, and bank. She decided that Afterglow wasn't too far behind the times.

Everybody she met greeted her in some way, and she received many a hearty, "Welcome to Afterglow." Months later when Hester would ponder her sojourn in Afterglow, she would always remember this midday walk as the time when she saw small-town America at its best. Little did she know then that she was destined also to see a small town at its worst. But since she did not suspect that on her first day in Afterglow, she enjoyed the walk.

She looked with appreciation at the three-story Grand Hotel across the street from the abandoned train station. Built of red brick in the Renaissance Revival style, the hotel was by far the most pretentious building in town and Hester thought what a pity to have it vacant, but realized that the small motel she had seen down by the covered bridge could probably house Afterglow's few transients.

An elderly man passing by paused and said to her, "The hotel was built in 1915 to take care of train passengers. The ballroom on the second floor is unique, with fancy carvings, velvet draperies, and old-country murals painted by an Italian who came here to work in the woods. He wasn't any good at lumbering, but he sure had a talent with the brush. My father said the dances they used to have there were a sight to behold."

"I suppose the building would need a lot of repair now."

"Not too much, ma'am. Probably some cleaning and painting would do wonders. Good day to you," he said as he tipped his hat and went on his way.

The street ended abruptly as the valley narrowed leaving only enough room for the railroad, long since abandoned. Hester's eyes followed the path of the ancient steel rails to a branch line that curved up the mountain about a mile down the valley before the main tracks entered a tunnel.

She turned and continued her walk on the opposite side of the street and, after she passed the city hall and the newspaper office, she wandered down a side street toward a set of low buildings on the riverbank. HARDWOOD FURNITURE FACTORY was written in faded letters over the door of one of the buildings. Hester peered through the windows, but she saw nothing, and abandoned further investigation when she stuck her face into a mass of cobwebs.

The brisk walk had warmed her and Hester unzipped her parka and sauntered toward the statue in the middle of Main Street. She took a notebook from her pocket and copied the inscription, only part of which she had been able to read when she had entered town.

HEZEKIAH BROWN, 1835-1915
FOUNDER OF AFTERGLOW
ENTREPRENEUR, PHILANTHROPIST, CIVIL WAR VETERAN
ERECTED BY THE GRATEFUL CITIZENS OF AFTERGLOW

Nearby, the sun highlighted the spire of a buff-colored brick church facing the river. Hester walked up the six steps and pushed on the door, which opened at her touch. The sanctuary looked as if it would seat more than 200 worshippers, which Afterglow may have had in its heyday. Stained-glass windows depicted famous episodes from the Bible and the vaulted ceiling and the pipe organ were reminiscent of European cathedrals. Hester wondered how a small town could have financed this magnificent church until she saw the plaque in the foyer.

This House of Worship is Dedicated to its Benefactor,
HEZEKIAH BROWN,
WHO BEQUEATHED A HALF-MILLION DOLLARS
TO THE CONGREGATION

Hester whistled. "Let's see," she calculated, "when did Brown die?" She checked her notebook: 1915. That had been quite a large bequest in that day, so it was little wonder that Afterglow revered its founder.

She eased down onto a pew. She had missed her daily devotional period this morning, so she sat in the quiet of the sanctuary for several minutes to allow her spiritual life to catch up with the rest of her body. She focused on the window depicting Jesus calming the angry waves, and the words below the scene, *Peace, be still,* helped to dispel her frustrations over the writing projects she had accepted.

Leaving the building more spiritually alert than she had been for months, Hester passed by Miss Eliza's boarding-house and she waved to a cane-supported elderly gentleman on the porch. Wind-wafted streams of condensation escaped from the vent pipe of the small house she had rented and she assumed the place was being readied for her. *Maybe my stint in Afterglow won't be so bad, after all.*

When her stomach and watch reminded Hester that it was past one o'clock, she entered the first restaurant she found and sat in a booth.

Menus were not available, but a middle-aged waitress called to her from behind the counter. "Chili with corn bread is today's special, but I can fix you a hot dog or a hamburger if you'd rather."

"The chili and corn bread sound good, and I'll take a large cola, too."

Two men sat at the counter with coffee cups before them. They looked at Hester curiously and spoke in friendly fashion. The door opened to admit a man she had seen at the centennial commission meeting and he headed her way.

"Mind if I join you, Hester?"

Hester smiled and indicated the bench opposite her while her mind floundered. *Which one was he?*

"I've been on a tour of the town this morning to get my

bearings."

"I saw you leave the church. Sorry I wasn't there to greet you."

Oh, yes, the pastor of the church, Ray Stanford.

"A beautiful building. I was amazed to find such grandeur in Afterglow until I noted the dedication plaque."

"After Brown remembered the church in his will, the congregation tore down the original log building and built the present structure."

"How long have you been the pastor?"

"Ten years. I'm a native of Afterglow. My family moved away when I was a teenager, but when I graduated from seminary, I applied for the position and was accepted. I'd missed the mountains."

The waitress hadn't even asked Ray what he wanted, but when she brought Hester's order, she sat a bowl of chili, corn bread, and coffee in front of him.

When he noted Hester's questioning look, he smiled. "I'm here every day at noon and I let Sadie choose my lunch. She knows what I like by now, anyway. I've been a widower for a couple of years and while I can rustle up a pretty good meal, I'm usually too busy to cook. We don't have many ministers in the area and I always have plenty to do."

"You know everyone in town, I suppose?"

"Just about. We don't have many newcomers."

"Do you know anyone by the name of Toby?"

"I don't believe so. Tommy Byrd used to live here, and I've known some Tonys and at least one Troy, but no Tobys. A friend of yours?"

"No, a friend of my mother's." His glance was speculative, but Hester changed the subject hurriedly to forestall further queries. "I'm full of questions after my morning's tour. Which house belonged to Hezekiah Brown?"

"Brown had a residence on the mountain close to his timbering industry. His heirs didn't choose to live there so the building is in ruins now. But back to your question about a Toby. Could it be a Tubby you're looking for? That's Mayor Stepp's nickname. Of course, now that he's our eminent mayor, we try not to use that name in connection with him."

Hester lifted a hand to her burning face and sipped hurriedly on her cola. *Just my luck to have Mayor Stepp turn out to be my father.* She would have to check that signature again.

Clint Noffsinger entered the restaurant and moved toward them. Ray scooted over in the seat and Clint sat beside him.

"Through for the day?" Ray asked.

"Yes. The presses are rolling so I've done all I can do."

The waitress brought Clint a cup of coffee and he smiled his thanks at her.

"Hester was wondering about Brown's residence. If you and Belle don't have plans for the rest of the afternoon, let's take her up there."

"I've walked for three hours this morning and I doubt I could climb a mountain," Hester said.

"You won't have to walk," Ray assured her. "Both of us have four-wheelers. I use mine about as much in my work as I do the truck."

"Then that sounds like a good idea to me. I need to learn everything I can about Brown, and I feel pressured to start on this research immediately."

"I'll phone Belle and see if she can arrange for a babysitter." Clint moved to the telephone placed conveniently on the food counter. When he returned, he took a final swig of his coffee and said, "She can go. We'll meet you at the trail head in a half hour."

Ray stood up and helped Hester with her coat. "You can ride that far with me, if you like, Hester, so you won't have to walk up to Clint's."

They left the restaurant together and took the short walk to the parsonage adjacent to the church. The four-wheeler was parked in Ray's garage, and Hester looked at it with some misgiving while Ray put a heavy cushion behind the driver's seat and loaded the vehicle into his pickup. The thing looked like a glorified motorcycle and she had always been afraid of motorcycles.

"We'll drive down the valley for a few miles before we take to the woods. It's illegal to drive four-wheelers on the highway so we have to travel partway in the truck."

Her companion wore a red plaid jacket, blue jeans, a red cap, and heavy leather boots. She smiled when she remembered her first impression of him.

"You surely fit into the surroundings. I suppose this isn't very flattering, but you look more like a lumberjack than a preacher."

His dark eyes gleamed with laughter. "What's a preacher supposed to look like? Do you expect me to dress in a clerical collar and robe all the time? Come to church Sunday and you'll see me as the stereotypical minister, but I interact with the natives better if I dress as they do. Besides, I prefer casual clothing."

"I hope you haven't adopted the tactics of the first missionary here. Didn't Miss Eliza say he invaded the saloons with a gun in one hand and a Bible in the other to gather a congregation?"

"I haven't gone that far yet, but I've been tempted."

Ray bypassed the covered bridge and traveled along a road that followed the meanderings of the river. Trees and bushes crowded both sides of the road that was hardly more than a trail.

"You will notice," he said, "that all of these trees are small. Years ago these mountains were stripped bare by the timber industry, but slowly new trees took root."

"Didn't the industry have a reforestation policy?"

"That concept was unheard of then."

After a short drive, Ray pulled into a turnout beside the road and unloaded the four-wheeler. Clint and Belle arrived in a few minutes.

"This was a good idea, Ray," Belle said. "Ina and I have gotten on one another's nerves today. It was a relief to farm her out for a few hours."

Belle straddled the back of Clint's four-wheeler when he unloaded it, and Ray indicated that Hester should ride behind him.

"We'll travel over some steep areas so you need to hold on to me. Don't drag your feet; put your arms around my waist and keep them there. I don't want you to fall off."

Noting her look of alarm, Ray chuckled and said, "There isn't any danger if you're cautious, but I want you to hold on."

When she locked her arms around his muscular waist, he said, "Not that tight. I have to breathe."

With a roar of his vehicle's engine, Clint disappeared into the forest ahead of them. Hester loosened her hold a little but kept her hands linked tightly as Ray left the clearing and steered the four-wheeler along an old logging road that wound upward through the woods over steep, rugged terrain. After Hester took one look through the barren trees and saw the river spiraling far below them, she shut her eyes and buried her face on Ray's back.

Not until the vehicle came to a sudden stop did she open her eyes. "Are we there?" She said breathlessly, looking around for some buildings. Ray helped her off the vehicle, but her legs wobbled and she leaned against the four-wheeler.

Belle rushed to her. "Are you sick?"

"I'm sorry to be so foolish, but I haven't been in mountains before. I feel dizzy and my ears are plugged. Your voice sounds far away."

"A perfectly normal reaction when you're unused to high altitudes. I should have thought of that," Ray apologized. "We came up several hundred feet quickly. Swallow several times and your head may clear."

"I had the same reaction when I first moved here," Belle encouraged.

Hester closed her eyes as Clint explained, "We're on a ridge now and we won't be doing any more climbing. This is where Brown's first sawmill was located and there are still remnants of it lying around. The house isn't far away. When you feel up to it, we'll investigate."

Perhaps the promise of no more climbing helped, for when Hester opened her eyes she felt almost normal.

Ray and Clint led the way into the nearby forest to the site of several ramshackle log buildings.

"The wood hicks spent months in the forest, so logging companies provided accommodations for them," Clint explained. "Brown had bunkhouses and mess halls for his crews. This long building was the bunkhouse, and I imagine the smaller structure was where the men ate. The cook was usually the best paid employee in the timber industry, for if the wood hicks didn't have good food, they would leave."

"Brown had camps all over these mountains, but this was the first site and where he had a sawmill, as I understand it," Ray added.

Stumbling over one of the many stumps protruding from the ground, Hester said, "After so many years, wouldn't you think these stumps would have deteriorated?"

"Brown's crew probably worked here no more than seventy-five years ago and it takes longer than that for all evidence to disappear," Ray explained. "Besides, after Brown died, other companies moved in and cut the smaller trees."

"I wish I could have seen these woods when they were full of virgin timber," Clint commented. "I've seen pictures of stumps big enough for a man to lie on and take a nap."

Large timbers marked the pit where the sawmill had been situated, and the steam engine stood in the spot where it had been abandoned years ago. A rusty circular saw leaned against a tumbledown building. As they walked around the deserted site, they saw the wreckage of axes, crosscut saws, and cookware left behind by the wood hicks.

"It's rumored that this site will become a monument to the timber industry if the state park becomes a reality," Belle said.

From the sawmill they walked for about fifteen minutes to Brown's residence on a promontory overlooking the town of Afterglow. Even when it was new, the house would have been unostentatious. They stepped up onto the unstable porch and pushed aside the sagging door to enter the spacious living room. The kitchen and dining area were to the rear of this room, and three bedrooms stretched out in an ell to the right of the kitchen. Dried grass, nuts, and animal droppings indicated that the dwelling had become a habitat for wildlife, but the wallpaper was still intact except for one corner of a bedroom that had been damaged by moisture from a leaky roof. The outbuildings had crumbled until only one, apparently a stable, was still standing. Hester ventured to the edge of the mountain for one quick look at the valley and scurried back to the safety of level ground.

"I don't know why that valley would appear familiar to me," she said. "Belle, you must have done a great job describing it. It's a beautiful setting for a town."

"Brown built his house here because he liked the view, or so I've heard," Clint said.

"I assume he was married. Did he have a large family?" Hester questioned.

Ray smiled. "We don't know. That's another thing we hope you'll find out." Hester groaned and he added laughingly, "You're going to be a busy woman if you do everything we think about."

"There's a family cemetery somewhere on this mountain, but I don't know where it is," Clint said. "Probably old Mr. Byrd knows. If you find it, that will give you some family information."

"Is Hezekiah Brown buried in that cemetery?"

"I think so," Ray told her.

"We don't have time to hunt for the graves today, but we'll help you find them later," Clint promised.

Though Ray drove slowly, Hester found the ride off the hill as terrifying as the ascent, but she had made up her mind to get over it. She had committed herself to a task in the mountains, and she had to shape up. When they returned to Afterglow, Ray drove up the hill and let her out in front of the Noffsinger house. Her ears roared and she heard his voice from a distance. Still a bit dizzy, she held on to the truck door when she stepped from the cab.

"Thanks. Today has been a good orientation to the area."

"Sorry about the dizziness. You'll soon become acclimated to the altitude."

When Hester reached her room, the first thing she did was to unlock the case that contained the Toby letter. The unpleasant thought that Mayor Stepp might be her father had been in the back of her mind all afternoon. She scanned the signature carefully. The message had been written in pencil and the letters were smudged and it was possible that second letter could be a *U* instead of an *O*, but if that were the case, the signature would be *Tuby,* not *Tubby,* which encouraged her considerably.

Why did the postal department have to find this letter? she moaned inwardly.

❧

The next day, after asking directions from Clint, Hester headed for the county seat twenty miles away. She wanted to begin her research with the courthouse records and, since Miss Eliza had sent word that she could move into the apartment tomorrow, today seemed like a good time to take the trip. She left immediately after breakfast.

Hester had no trouble spotting the courthouse situated on a wide lawn, and in the clerk's office she looked first among the recorded property deeds and survey plats of the towns. At noontime, she still did not have all the information she searched for, so after breaking for a sandwich and coffee, Hester reentered the courthouse to work for another two hours. Seated at the long table with more than a dozen deed books scattered around her, Hester leaned back in perplexity. Somehow the facts she sought kept eluding her, and wanting to cross the mountain to Afterglow before dark, she decided to return another day.

She stacked the books in one spot, picked up her purse, and started toward the door, which opened to admit a tall, handsome blond man whose face widened into a grin when he saw Hester.

My highway stalker!

She retreated into the room and shouted, "How dare you follow me this way!"

Surprise flitted across his face and he plunged his hands into the pockets of his neat, navy trousers, his eyes narrowed to a frown. "Lady, believe it or not, I never expected to see you again." He moved toward her and she glided behind the table. "Let's sit down and talk this out. It's just too much of a coincidence that we keep encountering one another. Maybe we should become acquainted."

"Are you sure you aren't following me?"

The blond-haired Apollo raised his right arm, and his eyes were laughing again. "Scout's honor."

Hester hesitated to be drawn into a conversation with him, although she could not help wondering why their paths kept crossing. She perched on the edge of a chair and favored him with a stony stare.

"Okay, I'll go first," he said. "My name is Kyle Trent. I'm an attorney, live in Harrisburg, Pennsylvania, marital status. . . unattached." He waved his arm toward her, indicating it was her turn.

"I'm Hester Lawson, journalist, live in Detroit."

He regarded her, his eyebrows raised in a questioning manner.

"Unattached, too," she admitted reluctantly.

"When I first saw you, I was returning from a business appointment in Pittsburgh. A week before that, my plans had already been made to come here and check some wills and deeds. I'm not following you; my business is perfectly legitimate. What is your reason for being here?"

Hester hesitated, not wanting him to know how long she would be in the region, but she finally said, "I'm on assignment now in the town of Afterglow."

He laughed delightedly. "Really! I have some business interests in Afterglow, too, and if you see me there, don't entertain the wrong idea. I planned this trip weeks ago."

"A likely story," she said.

"You're the most suspicious woman I've ever met. Do you consider your charms so wondrous that one fleeting look would cause me to follow you to the ends of the earth?"

Hester stood and started toward the door.

"Answer one more question before you leave. What kind of an assignment do you have in Afterglow?"

"Not that it's any of your business, but I'm doing research to compile a history of the town for its centennial celebration. I've been checking property lines today. The residents know so little about their town that I started my research with basic information. They don't even know why the town was named Afterglow."

"Oh, I can tell you that! When the founder of the town first entered the area, he stood on a high peak and looked westward. It was late in the day and the sun had already set, but the afterglow lightened the western horizon and cast its burnished hues on the valley where he eventually established a town. Hence, the name Afterglow."

"Are you making that up?"

He frowned. "Do I look like a man who would spoil a town's image and its heritage by offering erroneous facts?"

Hester looked intently at his firm chin and straight mouth. Somehow she envisioned that the expression in his unflecked blue eyes was reminiscent of the aggravating way Rhett Butler had often regarded Scarlett O'Hara. Yet, her pulse vibrated with an unaccustomed emotion.

"Yes," she said deliberately.

"Then run along, Miss Suspicious. You can search out the information by yourself. See you in Afterglow."

four

Hester braked steadily while going down the sloping hill until she reached Main Street where she drove left two blocks to the Byrd property. She was making this move reluctantly and she could not understand why. She certainly did not want to live with Belle and Clint the better part of a year, so what was her problem? Perhaps it was because she had never lived alone but, as she negotiated the narrow driveway and parked in front of the tiny house, she felt that her hesitation had to do with the dwelling itself. She mentally chastised herself and credited her qualms as "woman's vapors," as her Kentucky grandfather used to express it.

Whatever the cause, she breathed easier when Ray Stanford came out of the Byrd house and called in his booming voice, "I'll help carry your luggage." He took two of the heavier suitcases, and since he went in the house ahead of her, she did not hesitate about entering. Ray's tall, compact body dwarfed the living room and he measured between his head and the ceiling.

"Not more than four inches of clearance," he said with a laugh. "I was in this apartment when Tommy lived here, but I wasn't as tall then."

"It's much smaller than I'm used to, and I can think of many ways to make it more livable if I were going to live here long, but for a few months, I'll take it as it is. Except I will need a desk. Is there a furniture store in town where I can buy one?"

"I doubt that's necessary. Probably Miss Eliza has a desk to lend you. She keeps a backlog of furniture so she can fit up rooms the way her guests want them. Ask her before you buy one."

"Set everything in the living room and I'll organize it later," Hester said. When they had emptied her car, the two of them crossed the twenty feet to the back porch of the Byrd house and entered the kitchen where Miss Eliza was preparing pies for baking.

"Welcome, neighbor," Miss Eliza said. "Feel free to eat with us until you're settled," she offered.

"I'm going back to Belle's for dinner tonight," Hester said, "and I'll buy a supply of groceries today, but I'd love to eat with you occasionally."

When Ray inquired about a desk, Miss Eliza said, "We have some desks in the attic. Wait until I put these pies in the oven and we'll go look at them. Pour yourself a cup of coffee, Reverend, and get one for Hester. You're welcome to some of the nut bread in that plastic container."

Hester sat at the oilcloth-covered round table, placed two slices of nut bread on a napkin for Ray and took one for herself, while Ray brought two cups of coffee. Hester heard a cane tapping down the hallway and a white-haired, wispy old gentleman entered the kitchen, his body bent double over the cane.

Ray stood and held a chair for him. "Mr. Byrd, this is Hester Lawson, who's doing some work for the centennial commission. Hester, meet Everett Byrd."

Hester reached out her hand and Mr. Byrd pressed it weakly with trembling fingers.

"Larson, did you say? There used to be some Larsons in Afterglow."

"No, it's Lawson," Hester said loudly and she spelled the name for him.

Ray brought another cup of coffee for Mr. Byrd.

"I hope you'll share your recollections of the early days in

Afterglow for the history," Hester said loudly.

"I was born five years after this town was founded and I should remember a lot, although my memory ain't so good anymore."

"You remember the Hartwells, don't you?" Ray asked.

"Yeah. As a little tyke, I remember going to Sunday school in that chapel car of theirs. They had a little pump organ and Mrs. Hartwell played it while we sang. It was a funny looking church. . .just had two rows of seats, but it was long. We boys would sneak to the back seats and play around, and our mothers up front didn't know what we were doing."He paused and it was obvious that his memories dwelt fondly on that period in his life.

"But my monkeyshines stopped," the old man continued, "when I found the Lord and I started sitting up front in the Amen corner. Sorta hated to see the old chapel car move away, but when we had a church building and congregation, it was time for the Hartwells to move on to another field."

Miss Eliza pushed three pies into the oven, removed her apron, and motioned toward the small set of steps ascending from the kitchen. "We'll go up to the attic now."

"Huh?" Mr. Byrd cupped his ear.

"I wasn't speaking to you, Father. We're going to the attic to look at some furniture."

Miss Eliza spoke in her normal voice and Mr. Byrd nodded, which made Hester believe that he was not so deaf as she had thought. . .a point she must remember when she interviewed him.

Miss Eliza ascended the two flights of stairs quickly and motioned them into an attic that contained a hodgepodge of furniture, boxes, old clothing, and discarded dishes, all covered with cobwebs and dust.

"I come here only when absolutely necessary," Miss Eliza explained. "I don't know what to do with this accumulation, so I ignore it." She pointed to a handsome oak desk with a rolltop. "That item belonged to my father, who gave it to my nephew. For some reason, the top won't slide anymore, so I brought it to the attic."

Hester examined the many pigeonholes above the wide, flat writing surface. The extension slides worked well and she could see the utility of the six large drawers, as well as the card racks and the letter drops, but the roll top was stuck about six inches from the top and would not budge.

"I wouldn't have to close the desk, I suppose, and it would be useful, but will it be a problem to move downstairs?"

"We brought it up," Miss Eliza said crisply, "but by the front steps."

When they examined the other desk, a huge, flattopped walnut piece that had once been in the furniture factory, Hester decided to use the oak desk.

"Clint and I will move it for you," Ray offered.

Miss Eliza pointed to several boxes on the walnut table. "Those are records brought from the furniture factory, Hester. You may find them useful. In fact, there's an accumulation of artifacts up here that deal with town history. Look through them whenever you want."

ता

Hester spent the rest of the day unpacking her winter garments. Those that she would not need until spring and summer, she left in the boxes and shoved them under her bed, since there wasn't any room for them in the closet. She hung the Thomas painting over the spot where she intended to place the desk and as she backed away from the wall to be sure the painting was straight, she stared at it in amazement.

"What a coincidence!" she said aloud. No wonder she had thought the local river valley seemed familiar. She had been looking at it for years in her painting, *Winter Serenity*. Of course, there were differences, noting a boat dock in the foreground, and there was no covered bridge in the painting, but the high mountains, the narrow river valley, and the railroad disappearing into the distance were similar. Why were there so many coincidences lately?

She hung the embroidered sampler over the kitchen table and read aloud, "In all thy ways acknowledge Him and He shall direct thy paths." She was beginning to feel at home now.

Hester walked to a nearby store, bought enough groceries for a few days, and stored them in the kitchen cabinets. Then, noting that dusk was creeping over the town, she donned her coat and walked to the Noffsinger residence. She was panting when Belle opened the door to admit her.

"I'm still not used to this altitude," Hester said. "A little walk like that shouldn't make me gasp for breath."

Clint and Ina were nestled in a big chair watching cartoons, and he laughed. "You're doing the right thing, though. Keep walking and your lungs will soon expand to take in this light air."

"That's the reason I walked, and I'll walk to the centennial meeting, too. I refuse to become a victim of fresh mountain air."

"Sit down," Belle invited. "Dinner won't be ready for a few minutes. How did your moving-in go today?"

"I'm in," Hester said, "and that's about all I can report. It will take a few days to become accustomed to the plumbing and the kitchen stove. I used an electric stove in Detroit, so I'm having trouble with the gas."

"You'll soon adjust. I had the same problem when I moved to Afterglow."

"Miss Eliza has a desk I can use and there are several boxes of records in the attic that she thinks will be helpful in writing the history."

"The Byrds are an interesting family," Belle said.

"I met Mr. Byrd today and I keep hearing about Miss Eliza's nephew. Are there any other relatives?"

"No. The line is about to run out. Miss Eliza had only one

sibling—a brother," Clint answered. "He and his wife both died several years ago, leaving one child, Tommy. Mr. Byrd and Miss Eliza raised the boy, but he's never married."

"He apparently doesn't live here. I didn't suppose a native ever left Afterglow."

Clint laughed. "A few do and Tommy was one of them. I knew him when I was a boy, although he was probably twenty years my senior. He went into service and then came home for another year or two—that's when he lived in the little house—but he left then to look for work. I don't know where he is now."

"Ray volunteered your help in bringing a desk from the attic to my dwelling."

"We'll do that tonight after the centennial meeting," Clint agreed.

"I'm going with you," Belle said. "The mayor wanted all of the committee chairpersons to be at the meeting and report. I have a sitter coming to stay with Ina. I haven't been out of the house all day, so I'll enjoy a walk to the town hall."

❧

Hester and the Noffsingers were the first to arrive at the council chamber, but in a short while most of the seats around the large oval table were filled. With his usual fanfare, Mayor Stepp called the meeting to order. "We'll start with committee reports first and then take action on any items of business we have. Belle, what do you have to tell us?"

"We've advertised in the *Courier* for participants in the craft show and sale. About fifty people say they will come. Most of them are from this county, but we do have a few out-of-staters. I've made arrangements to use the first floor of the Grand Hotel. We'll need volunteers for cleaning the building but we can arrange that later. The Fourth of July weekend seems suitable to those we've contacted."

"What about the log raft ride?"

A middle-aged man, dressed in a dark business suit stood.

Hester recognized him as the city attorney, Alex Snead. "The logs will be delivered and dumped in the river by the first of May. There are still a few old-time wood hicks who remember how the logs were roped together to make rafts, and they'll give us some advice on how to maneuver our little flotilla. Logs are expensive and we're planning to build only two rafts, which will accommodate approximately twenty-five people, so we must think of someway to choose who's going to ride. And it might be a good idea to pray for a lot of rain. If the water level is low, we can't take a raft downriver between here and the county seat without wrecking on the rapids."

"Should be enough water in May, I would imagine," Ray said.

"Hopefully," Snead said, "but there hasn't been much snow on the mountain this winter."

"I can't wait any longer to give my report," Miss Eliza said, her brown eyes snapping with excitement. "You know we've been disappointed so far in our efforts to contact any descendants of Hezekiah Brown but just this evening, I received a telephone call from his great-grandson. He's arriving in Afterglow tomorrow and plans to stay in the area for a month or so. He has inherited the land that Brown owned in this county."

"Well, I say, Miss Eliza, that's wonderful news!" Mayor Stepp shouted and his arms waved wildly. He pranced around the table. "I'll wager he's here to arrange for the Brown land to be converted into a state park. I tell you, folks, Afterglow is facing the dawn of a new day."

One by one, the committee chairpersons gave their glowing reports until it was Hester's turn. She knew the information she had to deliver might have the effect of an exploding bomb, but she was determined to be nonchalant in her statements as if she were not concerned.

With beaming face, the mayor turned in her direction. "And

now, Miss Hester, we want to hear from you. Naturally, you haven't been here long enough to accomplish much, but we would like your opinion of our fair city."

"Oh, I've been very busy. Thanks to Mr. Stanford and the Noffsingers, I've visited Hezekiah Brown's house and his millsite, and I spent several hours in the courthouse yesterday. I'm rather puzzled about something I found there, or rather that I didn't find, so perhaps you can enlighten me. Where can I find a record of Brown's transfer of this land to the town of Afterglow?"

"Why, at the courthouse, of course," Alex Snead said.

"It isn't there," Hester stated. "I found the record where Brown had bought two thousand acres of land and where he had leased several acreages. Then, in later years, there are deeds of transfer from one property owner in Afterglow to another, but nothing to show that Brown ever relinquished his claim to the land where this town is located."

"Why, that's impossible," Mayor Stepp said and he drummed his fingers on the desktop. "Impossible."

"I don't know, Mayor. People a hundred years ago were apt to be careless in their property transfers," Snead said.

"I may have overlooked the record, but I don't think so, for I've had some experience in tracing deeds. Perhaps Mr. Snead can do some checking."

"I hope you haven't publicized this, Miss Lawson," the mayor said.

"This is the first time I've mentioned it."

The mayor swept the group with a stern glance. "And I trust the rest of you will remain equally silent. Of course, the record is there. Miss Lawson just didn't find it."

Hester judged that the mayor's formal use of her name indicated that he was unhappy with her report.

৵

Later, Ray Stanford joined the Noffsingers and Hester as they walked toward Hester's house.

"You certainly opened up a can of worms, Hester," Clint said and he laughed loudly. "Where do you think that record is, Ray?"

"Hard to tell. I don't remember that there has ever been a fire that destroyed county records. With all the moving around before the present courthouse was built, I'd just as soon think that a deed book has been lost."

"They seemed to be continuous," Hester said. "Anyway, I've tossed the ball to Attorney Snead's court. He'll have to take it from here. Obviously, Mayor Stepp is displeased with me, and you'd warned me, Clint, that he would try to suppress unpleasant things."

"He might try," Ray said, "but everyone in Afterglow will know about your report by noon tomorrow."

"You don't mean it!" Hester said.

"I do mean it," Ray said with a laugh. "The phone lines are probably doing overtime right now."

Belle went home to relieve the baby-sitter, but the two men accompanied Hester to the Byrd residence. It was almost midnight before they had the bulky desk moved from the attic and situated in the small house.

Ray looked closely at the *Winter Serenity* painting. "Wonder where Miss Eliza got this picture of the valley? I didn't notice it when I carried in your luggage."

Hester laughed. "That's an I. M. Thomas original that I brought with me. I was in one of his art classes at my university. I, too, think it looks like a local scene, but I suppose not, for he just painted it freehand in a landscape workshop."

"An amazing likeness," Ray said. "I've heard of Thomas but I hadn't seen any of his work."

After they left, Hester spent another hour washing the dirt and grime from the desk and rubbing it with a soft wax. It was a beautiful piece of furniture and she tried to determine why the top would not slide, but her hasty inspection did not reveal the problem.

Hester still had not overcome her feeling of dissatisfaction with the apartment but she was too tired to care, so she changed into pajamas, turned out the light, and went to bed. Afterglow's few street lights were behind the large Byrd house so it was dark in the room. The silence was still disturbing but it did not bother her as much as it had last week.

&

Hester awakened early the next morning and, after a quick breakfast, she unpacked her computer and other writing materials and moved them into the desk. She brought a straight-backed chair from the kitchen and decided she was ready to work. It was hardly comparable to her office at the newspaper, but she had not expected this to be a luxury assignment.

When she started downtown, Miss Eliza stuck her head out the window and called, "Plan to eat dinner with us tonight at six o'clock. I want you to meet our founder's descendant."

"Thanks. I'll do that." Hester wanted to experiment with the gas stove a few more times before she tried to cook dinner. She even had trouble this morning regulating the flame to boil water for tea.

Before she arrived at the *Courier* office, Hester was stopped by three people asking about her courthouse research. Several residents passed her wordlessly but with malevolent stares, and one woman even said, "Miss, you'd be better off if you would tend to your own business. You needn't think you can put me off my property."

"Whew!" she said when she finally entered Clint's office. "I feel as if I've been through a blitz!"

"I've been talking on the phone constantly since I arrived at seven o'clock. Everybody is in a turmoil." With an amused grin, he leaned back in his chair.

"But why get so upset before Mr. Snead has checked into the matter? I'm sure there's some logical explanation. The only reason I mentioned it was to learn if anyone knew where I could find the early records."

"Oh, it will die down soon. What can I do for you today?"

"I want to start checking through those records you said were stored here."

"Would it be more convenient if I bring them up to your place? There's no heat on the second floor of this building and you would be uncomfortable. There are six or seven cartons and I can load them onto a dolly to bring to your house."

"That would be great."

Clint stood and said, "If you can wait a bit, I'll have someone bring them downstairs and I'll take them as you return to your apartment."

"I would appreciate a bodyguard. If looks could kill, the ones I received on my way down here would have put me in my grave."

Clint and Hester were stopped several times on the way back to the Byrd apartment and the story had enlarged until some of the far-fetched comments left Hester speechless. One man said, "Is it true that Mayor Stepp is trying to sell the town hall?" A woman shouted, "Nobody is going to put me off my property. I've got a deed to it." A child ran up to them and said, "I heard a big avalanche is going to bury the town."

When they arrived at the apartment, Hester silently helped Clint move the boxes into her living room, but she finally said, "I wouldn't have believed it if I hadn't experienced this. Belle had written me that in a small town no one ever had a secret, and now I believe it."

"There are many advantages to living in Appalachia and as far as I'm concerned, they outweigh the disadvantages. But there are some disadvantages. You've witnessed one of them this morning."

Hester spent the rest of the day filtering through some of the boxes, where she found a wealth of data for the history in the old newspapers and clippings dating from the early part of the century, as well as memorabilia such as political campaign signs, movie posters, high school annuals, and announcements of New Year's balls in the Grand Hotel. The ballroom was described as a fantastic place and she wrote a memo to herself to see it soon. Hester typed notes on everything she found, delighted to have started a nucleus for the history, her excitement mounting as she worked. And as she made notes, ideas kept surfacing for the drama; these she jotted down on a yellow note pad. She envisioned a backdrop that would show the valley in a primeval setting, and an idea popped into her head that she considered both daring and brilliant.

Hester looked on the back of *Winter Serenity* where I. M. Thomas's address was listed as a post office box number in New York. Would mail still reach him there after all these years? It had been eight years since she had attended his art seminar. Impulsively, she typed a short note to Thomas, introducing herself and explaining her current project, and requesting his help.

> *Would you think it too presumptuous of me to ask you to paint a backdrop for our performance? Your painting,* Winter Serenity, *reminds me so much of this area, and it would be wonderful if you could produce something similar for the backdrop. I'm enclosing photos of the town as it is now. Please let me know if you're available to take on this project and the fee you would charge.*

Hester searched through her luggage until she found the Polaroid camera. She would take a few pictures in the morning and send the results off to I. M. Thomas. The most he could do would be to say no.

Dirty and disheveled, she realized that it was five o'clock. She had not broken for lunch, and she surely did not want to miss her dinner. She showered, washed and styled her hair, and changed into a shimmering, beige satin blouse and a pair of black slacks. By then it was almost six o'clock, so she threw a

wool blazer over her shoulders and hustled up the back steps
of the Byrd home.

The aroma of warm food greeted her nostrils and she
sighed appreciatively. It had been a long time since her cereal
and toast this morning. A flushed and beaming Miss Eliza
was carrying food from the kitchen into the dining room.

"May I help you?" Hester asked.

"Bless you, no," Miss Eliza refused. "I want you to meet
Hezekiah Brown's relative. He's in the parlor with Father and
Reverend Stanford. Come along."

Hester followed Miss Eliza down the hallway. She recognized Ray's booming voice and the quavering tones of Mr.
Byrd. But whose was the other familiar voice? Before she
could determine that, Miss Eliza motioned her into the parlor.

"Mr. Trent," Miss Eliza said, "I want you to meet our town
historian, Hester Lawson. Hester, this is Kyle Trent, a direct
descendant of Hezekiah Brown."

Why am I always being thrown into this man's company?

Ray and Kyle Trent had risen when the two women entered
the room. Hester opened her mouth but no words were forth-
coming, and she watched Miss Eliza's exit with a feeling bor-
dering on panic.

Kyle, however, was not so surprised as she was and he
moved across the room and took her hand, favoring Hester
with a wicked gleam from his blue eyes. "It's my pleasure to
meet you, Miss Lawson."

"We hope you'll be able to help Hester unravel some of the
mystery surrounding your ancestor, Mr. Trent," Ray said.

"I'll be pleased to help Miss Lawson any way that I can but
unfortunately, I know very little about Hezekiah Brown."

Hester realized he was still holding her hand, so she
removed it abruptly and walked away from him. She observed
a curious expression on Ray Stanford's face, and her discomfiture must have been obvious. Kyle Trent apparently intended
to treat her as a stranger, so she tried to compose her features

and as pleasantly as she could, she said, "I will probably need some help, but I have done quite well in my research today using the materials that Clint has at the *Courier*. I've found many interesting facts but it's a time-consuming job."

She turned to Ray, who was dressed in a brown suit with matching shirt and tie. No hint of the lumberjack tonight! "The desk meets my needs exactly," she told him.

"If you'll come into the dining room, we'll have dinner," Miss Eliza announced from the doorway. "My maid is feeding the boarders in the kitchen."

Miss Eliza seated Hester to her left and Kyle to her right, so that they faced one another, and Hester was so annoyed that she considered leaving. Ray sat beside Hester and to the right of Mr. Byrd, who pronounced a blessing on the food in his faltering voice.

More than once through the meal, Hester was thankful for Ray, who kept the conversation going so that she did not have to speak directly to Kyle. When she met his gaze, his expression was as bland as milk toast but she sensed his amusement at her discomfiture in his aggravating blue eyes.

When Miss Eliza entertained, she dined in style, and the maid started with a steaming vegetable soup, followed by salad and a roast beef dinner. Dessert was apple pie a la mode. Though she had been hungry, the presence of Kyle Trent had dulled her appetite and to Hester the deliciously prepared food was as insipid as boiled water.

They moved into the parlor for tea or coffee and shortly afterward, Ray excused himself. "I have a visit to make," he said. "Are you going to be with us long, Mr. Trent?"

"Not long this time, but I do intend to be in and out of Afterglow quite often this year. I've rented one of Miss Eliza's rooms for several months. I wouldn't want to miss the celebration."

"We'll look forward to that," Ray said as he left.

When Miss Eliza stood to remove the tea tray, Hester said,

"I'll help you." Now that Ray's stabilizing presence was gone, she wanted to escape.

"No, you keep Mr. Trent company while I organize things in the kitchen. Father isn't much of a conversationalist after he's had his dinner." She nodded toward Mr. Byrd who dozed in his chair.

"I'd be happy to have Miss Lawson's company and I'll invite her to join me on a walk. I need some exercise after that delicious dinner."

Hester opened her mouth to refuse but instead she said, "A walk sounds good to me."

"Excuse me. I'll run upstairs for a coat," Kyle said and when he returned, Hester had put on her blazer. He opened the door for her and they walked down the steps in silence.

"Which way?" he asked.

"We can circle the town on Main Street in a half hour. Let's go to the right first," she said shortly.

Kyle laughed and Hester turned on him fiercely. "You're enjoying this, aren't you?"

"It does have its amusing side, you'll have to admit. You didn't do a good job of acting. I don't believe we fooled the reverend into believing we hadn't met before."

"I had no intention of fooling him, but there didn't seem to be any reason to mention our encounters. Are you really related to Hezekiah Brown?"

"There you go again! Are you just naturally suspicious of all strangers, or is it only me?"

She did not answer and they walked a half-block in silence.

"Yes, I'm Brown's descendant. I have proof of it, for I'm sure I'm going to need it."

"So that's why you knew how Afterglow received its name!"

"It's a legend that's been handed down in the family."

When they reached the statue of Brown, Hester said, "There is a memorial to your exalted relative."

"The fact that this town honored him is a surprise to me. I don't know why, but our family has never seemed to think much of the old boy. My mother told me that, when she was a child, Brown's children never mentioned his name."

"So you *don't* know much about him?"

"No, but I inherited the estate of my great-aunt and she probably had lots of things you might use in the history. If I don't return to Harrisburg soon, I'll have my sister check through her papers."

"I suppose I was foolish to take on this task, for the centennial commission keeps adding to my duties, but I'm committed to it now and I'm going to give it my best," Hester said, wondering why she was unburdening herself to this stranger who kept cluttering up her life.

"I'm curious about how they ever found you. Didn't you say you were from Detroit?"

She explained briefly about her friendship with Belle and why she had come to Afterglow. By then they had reached the end of town and Hester said, "We have to turn back now."

As they ambled along the deserted streets, Kyle said, "I had hoped to find a restaurant where we could stop for a soda and talk, rather than to be shivering out here on the street."

"I was up late last night and I want to go to bed."

"Where do you live?"

"In the little building behind the boardinghouse."

"Then we'll be neighbors, for I intend to stay at Miss Eliza's frequently."

Hester wondered if he intended to sell Brown's property for a state park, but she would not question him. He walked with her to the door of her apartment and he said, "I'd come in if I had an invitation."

"But I'm not going to invite you. In the first place, I have papers spread all over the living room and there isn't any place to sit. Besides, the people in Afterglow are gunning for me now, so I don't dare entertain a stranger after dark. I'm sure that isn't acceptable here."

"Why are they gunning for you?"

She hesitated. "I'd rather not say."

Unlocking the door, Hester said, "I suppose I should thank you for not revealing our previous meetings."

"No thanks needed. Before you go in, tell me something else. What were you looking for in those deed books at the county seat?"

She hesitated again. "I won't tell you, but I will say that's what made the citizens of Afterglow mad at me."

She slipped into her living room and closed the door.

five

The next morning, before Hester started sorting through another box of the old papers, she wrote an article about Miss Eliza's boardinghouse to send to her newspaper in Detroit. She walked down to the riverbank and took a few pictures, enclosed them in the Thomas letter, and stopped by the post office to mail her correspondence. A few of the people she met greeted her with disgruntled nods but, for the most part, she was ignored. She encountered Mayor Stepp in the post office.

"You've certainly caused us a problem, young lady. Our phone at the town hall didn't stop ringing all day yesterday."

Hester did not appreciate being treated as a child and, with a quick prayer to help her control her temper, she replied calmly, "I didn't cause any problem. I simply stated that I hadn't found a record of the land transfer in the courthouse and asked where I might locate it. The matter shouldn't have been leaked to the public until Mr. Snead checked it. Apparently the commission members discussed it because I didn't mention it to anyone. How many people did *you* tell?" she asked pointedly.

The mayor harrumphed several times. "I thought it was my duty to notify the council members of a potential problem."

"Many others must have considered it was their duty to pass the news around. I feel sure that the transfer was made and I think the record can be found. The incident has been blown out of proportion."

"In the future, please clear any questionable information with me before you report it publicly."

"If you remember, that wasn't a part of our contract. See you later, Mayor. I have lots of research to do."

Hester had no intention of allowing the mayor to pass on everything she considered for publication or she would never finish the research in time, but she would not argue about it this morning. She found it difficult to put up with his theatrics and she shuddered to think of the remote possibility that this man could be her father.

When she reached her house, Kyle Trent called her name from the second floor of the Byrd dwelling. He leaned from a window that overlooked her house, which meant he could watch every move she made if he so desired. She waved to him and went on into her apartment.

Dark green blinds and lace curtains served as a window covering, so Hester pulled down the blinds in her bedroom. She had not considered that the residents next door had a bird's-eye view into her windows. At night, she should remember to pull the other blinds, too, but she needed to keep them open during daytime for extra light. The bulbs in the ceiling lights and lamps furnished inadequate lighting.

The research was slow work, but she could not complain about the amount of information she had accumulated. Numerous articles dealt with the timber industry and not everything she learned was good. She stared in disbelief at pictures showing how the mountains were clear-cut, which in turn led to landslides. She soon discovered that Brown was unpopular with some of the residents because of his exploitation of the forest. One man in particular, Michael Ledman, had spearheaded a fight to stop Brown from leasing land.

While Hester was eating her lunch, a loud knock sounded at the door and she laid her sandwich aside.

A masculine-looking woman, carrying a briefcase, stood at the door. "Miss Lawson, I'm Geraldine Ledman. I'd like to talk to you."

"Come in. May I offer you some lunch?"

"No, thank you. I've already eaten."

"Then you won't mind if I finish my sandwich." Hester pushed aside some papers to make a seat for the woman on the couch. "I'll be finished soon."

When she returned to the living room with a glass of cola that she placed on an end table, Geraldine Ledman was riffling through the papers Hester had laid to one side.

"So, you're reading about the timber industry," Geraldine said.

"That and other things. Not knowing exactly what I'll need, I'm doing general reading."

"I live at the county seat," Geraldine stated, "and I have some information I want published in this history of Afterglow."

"I appreciate your interest," Hester said without committing herself to publish material she had not examined and wondering if the woman would be a help or a hindrance.

"I'm not sure you'll welcome it. My grandfather, Michael Ledman, was victimized by Hezekiah Brown, as were several other landowners in this area. He leased land from them at a minimal price, misrepresenting the facts, and then sold the timber at huge profits." She motioned toward the briefcase. "I have papers showing that several of the landowners filed litigation against Brown to recover what he had stolen from them but the issue was never resolved."

"And this is what you want in the history?"

"It is. If you'll agree to publish the material, I'll make copies of some of these documents." A shrewd look covered her face and she added, "I can't turn loose of these papers for I still believe that we have a viable case. I hear the Brown land is to be sold, and if so, we're going to block the sale until we're paid our just dues."

Wait until Mayor Stepp hears about this.

"I would appreciate having copies of the papers for I want to research every possible source before I start writing the manuscript, but I won't promise that I'll include your case.

The history is limited to two hundred pages, so I can't publish everything, but it's necessary for me to follow all leads."

Ledman handed Hester a card. "My telephone number is here in case you want to contact me. But, regardless, you'll be hearing from me again."

After the woman left, Hester checked the time and walked to the restaurant where Ray Stanford often ate his lunch. She peered through the window and saw him seated at one of the booths. He waved and motioned her inside. She stopped by the counter and gave an order to Sadie. "Just a piece of cherry pie and a cup of coffee, please."

"How's the research going?" Ray greeted her when she joined him.

"Slow, but rewarding. It's a filthy job, too, in more ways than one. Those old papers are covered with dust and cobwebs."

"I imagined as much," he said, smiling. "Your face is dirty."

She took a tissue from her pocket and rubbed it across her face. "My hands would have been, too, but I washed them to prepare lunch. I didn't take time to check my appearance before I left for I wanted to catch you here at the restaurant."

He smiled again. "That's flattering."

"Maybe not. I'm using you for my sounding board. Do you know Geraldine Ledman?"

"I know who she is but I've never met the woman."

"Do you have any idea why she would come to see me?"

His fingers tried unsuccessfully to smooth his unruly beard and his dark eyes sparkled. "Unfortunately, I have. She's made a pest of herself in Afterglow the past year or so after she found some old litigation papers that her ancestor had drawn against Hezekiah Brown. She's badgered Clint to publish her claims in the *Courier*, but he won't. There has been some publicity in the county seat newspaper, but no one has paid much attention."

"I did find some information in the old newspapers to support her claims. Should I ignore her?"

"Not as far as I'm concerned. I don't doubt that Brown did gain his wealth by unethical means and I know we can't sugarcoat our past, no matter how much the mayor thinks so. Praise without adversity makes mighty dull reading."

"She promised to send me copies of her papers and I'll decide what to do after I've read them. In the meantime, as I research, I'm jotting down possible scenes for the drama. Now I'm wondering if this controversy between Brown and the landowners might make a good episode for the drama. We'll need some conflict."

"Sounds good to me."

Ray and Hester left the restaurant together and he said, "Day after tomorrow is Sunday. May I look for you at church?"

"Certainly. Is Afterglow a strict Sunday town?"

"The stores are all closed but there aren't any blue laws nor a ban on recreation, if that's what you mean."

By nightfall, Hester had sorted through all the boxes and had separated into one large stack the items she wanted to give further attention. She stopped early enough to prepare a decent meal, and while she ate leisurely, she scanned the daily issue of the *Courier*, which had been delivered to her door, compliments of Clint. Kyle Trent's picture graced the front page and Clint's article seemed to bear out what Kyle had told her about himself. A knock sounded at the door. *Why can't I enjoy one meal without an interruption?* Frowning, she opened the door on the smiling face of Kyle Trent. She stared at him without a greeting.

"Aren't you going to ask me in?"

"I'm eating my dinner."

"I won't take it. I've already eaten at the boardinghouse."

"Oh, come on in then," she said ungraciously. She raised the blinds and opened the curtains, which she had previously closed for the night. When Kyle looked at her curiously, she added, "I'm trying to preserve our reputations so the locals won't suspect us of clandestine activities. Come on into the kitchen. I'm not usually so inhospitable, but my lunch was interrupted, too."

She motioned him to the seat opposite her at the table. "Do you want some tea?"

"Yes, please." She reached into the cabinet for a cup and set the teapot beside him. He looked at her plate of baked pork chops, sweet potatoes, green beans, and cole slaw. "You eat well."

"I'm a busy woman. I need to be fed," she said as she resumed her seat.

"Who interrupted you at noon?"

"You wouldn't want to know. What have you been doing today?"

"Driving around, viewing my estate. I've never been here before. As a matter of fact, I didn't realize my aunt owned this land until she died and left the majority of her estate to me."

Hester pointed to the newspaper. "I see the *Courier* gave you some space. You must be the only descendant of Brown they've been able to locate."

"I don't believe he has many descendants but, as I told you, some of his relatives won't claim him."

When Hester prepared her dessert, she said, "Would you like some frozen yogurt?"

"No, thanks. I had a huge meal at Miss Eliza's. But if you aren't too busy, perhaps you'll accompany me on another walk. That activity should be acceptable behavior, even in Afterglow. And speaking of walking, Mr. Byrd told me that there's a Brown family cemetery on the mountain. I'm going to look for it tomorrow. Want to come along?"

"I do want to visit that cemetery, but I'm not doing well in this altitude. Do you expect to walk all the way?"

"The old gentleman says you can drive partway in a car and then walk across the mountain to the Brown house and cemetery. I'm not sure that I want to rely completely on Mr.

Byrd's directions, though."

"Clint Noffsinger will know. After I wash the dishes, we can walk up to his house and ask him."

To her surprise, Kyle dried the dishes. Soon, Hester shrugged into a heavy coat for the walk to the Noffsingers'.

Clint had already met Kyle and was introduced to Belle. Kyle surprised Hester by picking up Ina and making an instant rapport with her. Ina hadn't even accepted Hester yet! He must have a way with children. *And women?* Hester wondered. Instinctively, her guard was up against Kyle Trent.

Answering Hester's query, Clint said, "I can tell you how to reach the logging site by taking a trail up the mountain, but I don't know where the cemetery is."

Tossing a rubber ball to the chattering Ina, Kyle said, "Mr. Byrd gave me some general directions. If we reach the house, I can probably find the cemetery."

"Drive west of town along the old railroad tracks until they disappear into a tunnel. At that point, turn left and follow an old logging road about a mile up the mountainside. It's a rough drive, so you won't want to take your car."

"I drove partway up that road today and made it all right."

Clint shrugged his shoulders. "Park your car near some dilapidated buildings, then cut across country through the forest on a small trail you'll see to the left. It's a mile and a half to the sawmill site, but it's steep climbing and before you come to Brown's homestead, you'll think it's twice that far. If we didn't have to go to the county seat tomorrow, we could go with you. But you can borrow my four-wheeler if you like."

Hester darted a glance at Kyle. "Have you ever driven a four-wheeler?"

"No."

"Then if I go with you, we'll walk. I was terrified when I rode up that mountain with Ray Stanford and he's an experienced driver."

"Be sure and wear serviceable shoes that have rough soles,"

Belle advised. "We'll lend you a backpack to carry a lunch and be sure to take water and first-aid items," Clint said.

"We'll be gone only a few hours, won't we?" Kyle asked. "Why should we need a first-aid kit?"

"Better to be safe than sorry," Clint argued.

They watched television with the Noffsingers, staying until they heard the eleven o'clock news. Since the weather forecast was for mild weather, they agreed to take the hike the next day.

"I'll pack a lunch," Hester said when they parted at the Byrd gate. "What time?"

"Nine o'clock, okay?"

"I'll be ready."

❧

The next morning, Hester held her breath as well as the sides of the seat more than once, before Kyle parked the Mercedes at the end of the road. He had driven through mud holes, crept over fallen logs, and subjected the automobile to abuse on the rutted trail. Some people might call it a road, but it was nothing more than a wide path.

She trembled when she eyed the trail winding upward through the forest. "I'm not sure I can go on. When I went up with the Noffsingers and Ray Stanford by vehicle, I nearly passed out."

"The altitude change won't bother you as much when we're traveling slowly. But if you have trouble, we'll turn around and come back," Kyle said calmly.

"Doesn't anything ever excite you?"

"You should see me at my best in front of a jury. I'm excited then. I'm the best trial lawyer in our area."

"Add conceit to the list of your faults."

"It isn't conceit to tell the truth."

He fastened the backpack over his shoulders. "Here goes," he said and saluted smartly. "Forward, march!"

Hester preceded him up the trail and it took two hours of twists and turns, panting and puffing before they finally reached the level area that Hester recognized as the Brown sawmill site.

They looked through the deserted buildings and Hester said, "The rumor is that state officials have talked of restoring this area into a museum to the lumber industry."

"They'll have to buy it from me first and, from the looks of these buildings, I question that any of them are restorable."

They moved on to the Brown residence and Kyle laughed when he saw it. "So this is my ancestral home. I thought Hezekiah Brown was rich."

"Perhaps the reason he was rich was because he didn't spend much on his residence. It would have been a good house for the early twentieth century though."

Kyle leaned against a crumbling porch post and looked at the vista spreading before them. "So here's where my ancestor stood when he named the town. Pity the place didn't live up to its name. There's not much of an afterglow about it now."

After they looked over the dwelling, Hester said, "I'm hungry. Shall we eat before we look for the cemetery?"

"Suits me. Let's sit on the step. It will be warmer here in the sunshine than inside the house."

Hester spread out the picnic lunch. "I haven't bought many groceries yet, so you'll have to be satisfied with tuna salad sandwiches, apples, and cookies. In addition to the big bottle of water, I brought along two containers of fruit drink. Belle also left a sack of trail mix in the pack, so we can eat that before we start back down the mountainside."

"I found out why the citizens of Afterglow are angry at you," Kyle said as he bit into a big Grimes Golden apple.

"Oh?"

"Mr. Byrd told me. I had an idea what it was, for after I saw you that day in the courthouse, I spent hours looking and I couldn't find any indication that Brown had ever given away the town site of Afterglow."

"It's a mystery to me, but I'm not a professional in tracing property titles. As an attorney, you should know how to look for that type of thing. What do you make of it?"

"Brown set up Afterglow as a company town, rather like the coal companies did. I don't believe he ever turned the land over to the citizens. When the timber industry declined, he just allowed them to keep their homes. And from what I make of it, I own the town of Afterglow."

Hester choked on a sip of fruit juice and stared at him. When she could speak again, she said, "That's ridiculous. What about squatter's rights?"

"Squatter's rights haven't been legal for a hundred years or so and wouldn't apply in this case. Normally, I wouldn't care who owned Afterglow, but I'm trying to sell this land to the state. They're interested but don't like having a town within the confines of the park."

"There's not much you can do about it, is there?"

"Maybe not, but I'm going to suggest that the city fathers relocate the town outside the park."

Hester laughed. "You wouldn't have a chance."

"I'm not so sure. If the state wants the land badly enough, they might put pressure on the residents. For the time being, I hope you won't mention that I'm aware of the situation."

"Never fear, for I'll be blamed for telling you about the missing deed anyway. I can hear the mayor's reaction. He's heard a rumor about this state park and he believes that will transform Afterglow into a tourist attraction."

They stored the remains of the lunch in the backpack and placed it inside the house.

"Now, let's look for the cemetery. Mr. Byrd said it was due north from the back door of the house. Let's see if I can take my bearings from the sun just like a true pioneer."

Kyle's bearings indicated that they would have to climb higher to reach the cemetery.

"Not another hill," Hester protested.

"Head bothering you?"

"Not particularly, but I'm not used to this sort of terrain. In Detroit, I jog or walk every day, but climbing is hard on my muscles. The skin on the back of my legs feels stretched as tight as a bowstring and my hip joints ache."

"I know. I felt the pull on my leg muscles while we were climbing. Why don't you stay here until I scout around? If I find the cemetery, I'll call for you."

"Since neither of us know anything about these mountains, we should stay together for we could easily become lost. I'll manage."

"Going back should be easy. Downhill."

"But a *steep* downhill and Belle warned me to be careful on the steep places. Oh, for some level land again."

"Do I hear a tremor of homesickness?"

"I know I'll never become a mountaineer. Let's find that cemetery."

The trail to the cemetery was indistinct, but possible to follow. To Hester's relief, the trail did not go uphill, but led around the mountainside to a small level spot surrounded by a dilapidated rail fence. The gate was secured with a rusty wire, so Hester and Kyle stepped through a broken-down section of the rails. Hester counted twenty granite headstones and several wooden slabs marking other graves.

"Here's the old boy's stone," Kyle said. Brown's marker was unpretentious, comparing meanly to the large statue of him in Afterglow. Kyle pulled away the dead weeds so that they could read the inscriptions.

Hezekiah Brown and his wife, Elizabeth, were buried side by side, adjacent to the graves of their two infant children.

"I believe he had three children who lived to adulthood," Kyle said, "and I'll try to find that information from my aunt's papers."

"This must be Hezekiah's parents," Hester said, pointing to a double headstone of a generation earlier. "From some of the information I've read, it seems his father moved into this area so he would be away from the slave owners in Tidewater, Virginia."

"Gives me a rather strange feeling," Kyle admitted, "to be standing where my ancestors walked. I wish I knew why my family didn't think much of Hezekiah Brown."

"I may know why," Hester said and she told him about her visit from Geraldine Ledman.

Kyle whistled. "So my ancestor was a crook! But that could be termed unethical rather than illegal. There must have been something else wrong with him."

"It's a pity this place has been neglected," Hester said as she pulled briars and undergrowth away from the plots. She took a notepad from her pocket and recorded the information from the tombstones. The graves in one section with names and dates cut into slabs of wood had no apparent connection with the Brown family nor with one another.

"No doubt these were some of Brown's workers," Kyle said. "I agree with you about the cemetery. If the state buys this property, I'll stipulate that they have to provide care for the cemetery. If not, I'll do it myself. If a man's spirit has gone to be with God, it doesn't matter much where the body is buried, but I don't like to see my ancestors' graves neglected like this."

Hester did not answer, but she was pleased to know that Kyle's spiritual priorities seemed to be in the right place.

As she plodded down the trail, tagging after Kyle Trent, Hester assessed the day's activities. Other than knowing where Hezekiah Brown was buried, she did not feel that she had accomplished much on her research. But, on a personal side, she had gained a better rapport with Kyle. He had been a great companion today.

six

Strains of the pipe organ greeted Hester as she entered Brown Memorial Church the next morning. Her church in Detroit did not boast a pipe organ, so the town of Afterglow had one up on her there. She sat on a seat near the back, although the sanctuary was sparsely filled. She soon felt a tap on her shoulder and Belle leaned over to whisper, "Come up front and sit with us."

Glad for their company, Hester entered another pew to sit between Belle and Clint.

"I took Ina to the nursery," Belle whispered.

As the organist built the prelude to a mighty crescendo, Kyle entered the church and sat opposite them. He smiled in her direction. Hester hated to see him sitting alone but she could not very well leave the Noffsingers to keep him company.

This morning Ray no longer resembled a lumberjack, for he made an impressive figure in his black robe. In spite of the vaulted ceiling of the church, his massive figure dominated the room throughout the service. The choir singing was mediocre and the congregation was sparse, but she could find no fault with Ray.

"In my research of the chapel ministry," he said, "I found a journal that Ivan Hartwell kept during his year at Afterglow. He listed his sermon texts and Scriptural reference for each Sunday. Starting today and until the end of our town's celebration, I will use Brother Hartwell's ideas. Today, the text is Romans 10:13-14: 'For whosoever shall call upon the name of the Lord shall be saved. How then shall they call on him in whom they have not believed? and how shall they believe in him of whom they have not heard? and how shall they hear without a preacher?'

"This is one of the greatest missionary texts of the Bible and one that Hartwell used to govern his actions when he first came into this area. The train that brought him to Afterglow was met by angry wood hicks, demanding that he move on. Although Hartwell was confronted with anger and violence, he persevered until he had the nucleus of a church in this community."

Ray proceeded to use the text and Hartwell's example to point out the need for a renewal of missionary activity in their town. In a final challenge to his listeners, he said, "Would God we had anger against our cause today, rather than the apathy that afflicts our friends and neighbors who have no concern for their spiritual welfare. During this year of celebration, I pray that we will not only remember the historical events of the past, but once again experience the religious zeal and fervor of our forefathers."

Kyle fell into step with Hester as she started down the aisle at the end of the service. "I'm leaving this afternoon. I've been away from my office for two weeks and I must go home to take care of the correspondence that has accumulated. I intend to be back for the council meeting ten days from now."

In a low voice, she cautioned, "You're going to stir up a hornet's nest. They'll run you out of town on a rail."

"Probably that's what they should have done to my esteemed ancestor instead of erecting a monument in his honor."

Hester stood aside to wait for Belle, who was visiting with everyone as she left the church. Kyle shook hands with Ray, smiled in Hester's direction, and ran jauntily down the steps. Afterglow would seem emptier after his departure; it had been comforting to know she was not the only stranger in town.

The following week passed quickly as Hester worked out a basic format for the history book. She visited dozens of homes with her tape recorder, asking residents to share their stories of the past. She also begged for old photos until she had hundreds of them. Although she was still shunned by a few people, most of them had decided that the absence of Afterglow's deed would not cause any problem and they had forgiven Hester's mention of it.

The most exciting event of the week was the receipt of a note from I. M. Thomas. On a small sheet of paper, he had scribbled an answer to her request.

>   *Delighted to do the backdrop for drama. No*
>   *charge. Will send in plenty of time for presentation.*
>   *I. M. Thomas*

In spite of his advanced age or perhaps because of it, Everett Byrd provided the most information about the timber industry. Hester made arrangements to meet him one afternoon after his nap. He eyed the tape recorder with alarm.

"I don't want to talk into that contraption," he insisted.

"You don't have to talk into it. You just recount your experiences and forget the recorder is here. My memory isn't so good as yours and I need this recording for accuracy."

"All right, young woman, what do you want to know?"

"Anything you can tell me about the timber industry in this area."

"Hezekiah Brown was the first one to start timbering here about a year before the town was started. His father had owned a little land in the county, but Brown moved away for a good many years. He said he never forgot the valley and he came back after he made his fortune elsewhere. He was the first, but we had a lot of timbering after Brown died."

"What did you do in the industry?"

"I started working for Brown when I was just a boy. We

didn't have child labor laws then. I could use an ax and a crosscut saw by the time I was twelve. I guess I did about anything that had to be done."

"Give me some examples, keeping in mind that I'm a city girl without any knowledge of lumbering."

"I can remember when there was virgin timber on these mountains. I've cut trees that measured six to eight feet through. We would have to make big notches all around the tree with an ax before we could saw it."

He stifled a yawn. Hester cleared her throat to alert him and he continued, "Before I started cutting trees, I helped the road gang build roads so the wagons could move in to gather the cut logs. When the mountain was too steep for a wagon to travel over, we sledded the logs down."

"What kind of trees were harvested?"

"Most any kind of hardwood, but during the thirties, we cut a lot of dead chestnuts that had been killed by a fungus blight. There were thousands of those chestnuts standing around on these mountains."

Mr. Byrd started to nod and Hester turned off the tape recorder until he had finished his nap. When he roused, she asked, "Tell me about some of the jobs you had."

"I did some swamping, but everybody had to do that. That's when the men cleared the forest of undergrowth and fallen logs to prepare the ground for skidding logs. None of us liked that, but it had to be done." He paused in his narrative and reflected, while the grandfather clock in the hallway chimed the half hour.

"I was a millhand for a few months. As offbearer, I took the waste wood and piled it up to use for fuel in the boiler to fire the sawmill. Once I was a ratchet man. That meant I rolled the logs down into the circular saw carriage. That was a particular job for I had to determine how the boards were cut into widths and lengths."

"Sounds like a hard job," Hester said as she turned over the tape in her recorder.

"It was, but I didn't like working around the sawmill, so I spent most of my time with a team hauling the logs off the mountainside and down to the railroad. I guess that was my favorite job. I like horses."

"Do you believe Brown was unethical in his dealings?"

"Maybe, but it took a lot of money to finance his work. If he was, he paid it back by remembering Afterglow in his will."

"Did you ever work in the furniture factory here in town?"

"No. It took craftsmen for that work. At first they made furniture, but it proved more economical to ship the lumber out of here and have the furniture made elsewhere. Mostly, they made knickknacks. It was never a profitable venture."

Hester also spent several days in Miss Eliza's attic where she found numerous ledgers, invoices, and memorabilia of the town's furniture factory. She secured a key from the real estate agent who had the property listed for sale and took a tour of the buildings. When the centennial commission met on Tuesday night, Mayor Stepp complimented Hester on her work, and she assumed he meant to let bygones be bygones.

"As I toured the factory yesterday, I thought it would make a great tourist attraction," she reported. "I envisioned using it as a training school for those interested in cabinetmaking or in producing small wooden items for sale. Do any of the craftsmen who used to work in the factory still live around here?"

"A few, I believe," Miss Eliza said. "But it would cost a lot of money to renovate the buildings and the factory closed in the first place because of lack of customers."

"It would have to start out on a small scale, making novelty items, for you would be appealing to a new kind of customer— the tourist. You could probably ask for a state or federal grant for expansion funds, especially if the area becomes a state park."

Even as she spoke, Hester wondered about the fate of Afterglow. Did Kyle have any possible chance of making them relocate the town? No doubt he had been working all week to shore up his defenses, determining if he had the legal clout to take over the town's land. If so, the old factory would never operate again.

When Clint smiled at her, she said, "And don't expect me to write up a grant application. If I accomplish what you've already laid out for me, it will be a miracle."

"You've opened up a new avenue of thought, Miss Hester," the mayor said, "and we'll take it under advisement."

"In the meantime, you might want to consider producing a few souvenir items for this year." She took two drawings from her briefcase. "I found these in Eliza's attic. They're sketches for a walnut vase and a curio shelf. It seems to me they would be easy to make and I believe that tourists would purchase them."

"The only person in town who could do that is Charles Benson," Miss Eliza said briskly. "That is, if you want to involve him in this celebration."

"Why not?" Alex Snead asked. "Just because he's the descendant of Aaron Benson doesn't keep him from being a craftsman."

"Since Aaron Benson has the distinction of being the only person to rob the local bank, he should be remembered someway. By all means, contact Charles Benson if we decide to pursue this project," Clint said.

❧

The next morning, Kyle returned and soon made his way to Hester's quarters. By now, she recognized his knock, which was a rat-a-tat rendition of "Shave and a haircut, two bits."

He entered at her invitation. "I come bearing gifts," he said. "I raided my great-aunt's files and came up with a collection of goodies on the Brown family. . .at least I hope they're goodies. I haven't read them." He placed the box he carried on the floor and perched on a chair near Hester's desk.

"What if I find something that isn't a 'goody'? May I publish it anyway?"

"Yes, as far as I'm concerned. Are you coming to the council meeting tonight to hear the fireworks?"

"Are there going to be some?"

"I wouldn't be surprised."

"I might as well come," she said. "I'll be blamed for leaking the information to you. You may have to make room for me on that rail."

"I can't think of more delightful company." He sauntered toward the door. "See you tonight. I have to check in with Miss Eliza and be sure she has enough food for me."

Hester quickly glanced through the packet of materials that Kyle had brought, noting with gratification that there was a picture of Hezekiah Brown and other members of his family. She intended to incorporate many old pictures into the history and there definitely should be some of the Brown family. She laid aside the packet when a knock sounded at the door.

A tall, thin man stood on the low step. He removed his cap to reveal a thatch of curly brown hair. "My name's Charlie Benson, ma'am. Miss Eliza sent me around to see you."

"Come on in. Did Miss Eliza tell you what we're considering?" He nodded and she handed him photocopies of the patterns of the vase and the curio shelf that she had made at the mayor's office.

"Could you duplicate these items if the commission decides to produce them? And could you teach others to make them?"

He whistled tonelessly while he studied the drawings. "Reckon I could, but it would take some time. If you're intendin' to have these ready to sell this summer, it's already too late to start."

"Perhaps you could have a supply ready before the big celebration in October."

"Reckon I could," he agreed.

"Will you make up a sample of these two items before the next centennial commission meeting? I'm sure the members will want to see a sample before they agree to spend any money."

After he left, Hester ate a light meal and hurried up the hill to the Noffsingers'.

"Come along to the council meeting with me tonight," she said to Clint. "I'm not at liberty to comment upon it, but Kyle Trent is going to drop a bomb on Mayor Stepp. As a newspaper editor, you'll want to be present."

"I always send the city editor to cover the council meetings, for they're usually humdrum," Clint said, "but I'll take your word for it and attend. Can you find a baby-sitter, Belle?"

"No, but I'll take Ina along. She had a long nap this afternoon, so perhaps she'll behave herself. If not, I'll bring her home."

&

When Hester and the Noffsingers entered the council room, there was no sign of Kyle, but Geraldine Ledman sat in the front row of the spectators' chairs. When Clint looked questioningly at Hester, she whispered, "I didn't know she was going to be here." If Geraldine made public any of the papers she had brought to Hester, this was going to be a lively meeting.

The mayor had already called the session to order and the clerk was reading the minutes of the last meeting when the door opened. Kyle slipped quietly into the room. He looked as sanctimonious as a saint and Hester was sure he had timed his entrance for this moment. He ignored Hester, much to her relief.

When the council finished its agenda relating to repaving Main Street, the mayor turned grandly toward the spectator section. "I see we have a few visitors tonight. Do any of you ladies or gentlemen have anything to say? It isn't customary to take up any unscheduled business, but we have no rule against anyone speaking."

Kyle nodded his thanks to the mayor and moved to center stage, or at least that's the way it appeared to Hester. She believed his comment about being the best trial lawyer in the area, for from the moment he stood, he commanded everyone's attention. Dramatically, his eyes roved the room, looking directly into the face of each person there. His attitude stunned the group to silence, and when the room was as quiet as a tomb, he said bluntly, "Would you have any objections to relocating the town of Afterglow?"

If it were a bomb, it did not make any noise, for no one said anything. In fact, even Hester, who had expected something of the sort, was stunned. He could have led up to the matter!

"As you know, I've inherited the land in this county that once belonged to Hezekiah Brown and, to the best of my knowledge, that includes the one hundred acres on which this town is situated. I've spent several days checking property records at the courthouse, and there is no record that Brown ever relinquished claim to this land."

The mayor and some of the council members cast angry glances toward Hester.

"I've heard that Miss Lawson made a similar finding, but I learned that after I arrived in town. She didn't tell me; I found out myself."

Mayor Stepp's face had turned a dusky red and he blustered, "Are you suggesting that you own this town?"

"Just the land it sits on; any improvements are yours. I simply want the land back as it was in my ancestor's time. That's the reason I suggested relocating the town. There's a site on the other side of the mountain that would make a good place for you. The buildings could be sent downstream on barges and the town could be reestablished in no time. Stuck up in this hollow, Afterglow will never amount to anything anyway."

"I don't believe a word of it," Mayor Stepp shouted. Turning to Alex Snead, he said, "Have you checked those deeds yet?"

Looking unhappy, Snead said, "Yes, I did, and I have to agree with Mr. Trent. There is no record of a land transfer."

"Even if there isn't," a council member said, "it's out of the question. . .ridiculous to expect us to move our homes. This town has been here for a hundred years! We're supposed to be celebrating the town's founding, not dismantling it."

"Afterglow is dying anyway. Why not turn your celebration into a big funeral and move?" Kyle asked with a smile.

"No, no, no!" Mayor Stepp shouted. "Afterglow is here to stay. There has to be some mistake. We'll try this in a court of law."

"Speaking of a law court," Geraldine Ledman said as she stood. "I, myself, have a suit to present. . .against the heirs of Hezekiah Brown. And I'm pleased you're here to represent them, Mr. Trent. I have evidence," she patted her briefcase, "that will show how your ancestor, Hezekiah Brown, defrauded the early residents. I represent the descendants of eight landowners who were duped by Brown into leasing their land to him. He not only gave them insufficient money but he exploited the forests. He was to cut only the large trees, but he clear-cut instead. We expect to be paid for our losses."

Kyle retained a smile on his face, but Hester could tell by the twitching nerve in his forehead that he was angry.

"If I can dish it out, I can take it," he said. "Bring on your lawsuit."

Mayor Stepp pranced back and forth in the room, wringing his hands. "Mr. Trent, Miss Ledman, you're ruining the image of this fair town." Turning to Hester, he continued, "And don't put a word of this in your history. What if the newspapers should get hold of this?"

"I do intend to publicize it. If you want tourists flocking to the town, they'll come in droves when they hear of this controversy. The public thrives on conflict; good news doesn't make interesting reading."

"I declare this council meeting adjourned," Mayor Stepp cried. Immediately, those present drifted into shouting, gesticulating groups. Geraldine Ledman approached Kyle, who observed her with a cynical smile on his face.

"It's time we were getting out of here," Clint said as he shepherded his family and Hester toward the exit. They paused on the street and he continued, "You go on home, Belle. I'm going to stop at the office and write up a news story for tomorrow's paper. Mayor Stepp's efforts to stop this will have as much effect as putting out a brushfire with a pot of tea."

"You said you would liven up things for us," Belle said to Hester, "but I don't need this much excitement. Coming home with me?"

"No. I'm going back to the apartment, write an account of this incident, then go to the county seat early in the morning and fax it to Detroit."

Hester had just written the headline, *SMALL TOWN'S CELEBRATION MAY TURN INTO ITS FUNERAL*, when she heard Kyle's knock at the door.

"Come in," she called, and when he barged into the room, she said, "I'm busy."

"And I'm elated," he said, throwing his coat across the couch. "Nothing excites me like a healthy controversy."

"If you're going to stay, open the blinds and curtains. And you'll have to be quiet until I've finished. I'm writing an account of this healthy controversy to send to Detroit."

"May I read it after you've finished?"

"Of course not. I don't need a proofreader."

"Let me ask you a question and then I'll leave. Do you still have those papers that Ledman woman gave you?"

Hester pulled out one of the lower drawers of the desk and handed him a file labeled, *Ledman Papers*.

"She brought me copies of quite a few things that she wants incorporated into the history. You can take the file with you but I want it back as soon as you've read everything."

He looked at the drawer full of neat files. "I see you're a well-organized woman. Did you bring this desk with you?"

"No, it's one that Miss Eliza had stored in the attic, but I surely like it. These big bottom drawers are just the right width for letter-sized files and I particularly like all the pigeonholes in the upper part. I may try to buy it from her and take it home with me if I can get the top to roll down. It's stuck in this position."

Kyle peered under the lid and he tugged on it. "A cabinet-maker could probably help you."

His suggestion had merit and Hester decided she would have Charlie Benson take a look at it. Kyle picked up his coat, tucked the file under his arm, and left.

❧

The month of February turned out to be a time of bickering for the whole town. One morning Kyle discovered that all four tires on his Mercedes had been slashed. Up until that time, he had not gotten angry, but the howl he put up when he discovered the mutilation could have been heard on the other side of the mountain.

The town divided into factions: those who favored the lawsuit Geraldine Ledman proposed and those who believed the town of Afterglow should be moved. Kyle and Hester figured in every dispute and they bore the brunt of everyone's ire. Only the Noffsingers, Byrds, and Ray remained friendly to them. On Sunday mornings, most of the disputants attended church, and Ray's sermons were designed to pour oil on the troubled waters of the town, but on Monday the citizens were arguing again.

In late February, an environmentalist group from the county seat appeared at a centennial commission meeting and demanded that the celebration be stopped. For how could they honor a man who had desecrated the forests and robbed his neighbors? This added predicament unnerved the mayor to such an extent that he burst into tears in front of the commission's members.

But tempers cooled off near the first of March when a heavy snowstorm isolated Afterglow from the rest of the world. The roads were closed and telephone service was interrupted when the wet, heavy snow snapped the utility lines.

The whole area looked like a giant Christmas card, with the evergreen trees decorated with heavy tufts of snow and cardinals nestling in their branches. The citizens forgot their differences and enjoyed the only snowfall of the winter. A small knoll below the town provided a gentle downhill slope for sledders. The river froze from bank to bank and bonfires along the riverbank each night illuminated the ice for the skaters.

Kyle was gone from Afterglow during the snowfall, but Hester enjoyed the day and evening activities, coming back to the apartment cold and wet from the snow, happily alive and vibrant. After a warm shower, she would bundle up in a heavy wool robe and pore over the notes she had made during the day. The history research was going well and she and Clint had made preliminary plans for the format and printing. True to her journalistic beliefs, she was painting Afterglow and Hezekiah Brown in their true colors, some black, some white. But, one night she encountered something in the packet of papers that Kyle had brought that threw her whole perspective off balance—she had uncovered a situation where it might be best to conceal the truth.

seven

Hester scrutinized the paper carefully, trying to figure if it could be a hoax, for it would be like Kyle to put in such a document just to discomfit her. But the paper was obviously old, and in Hezekiah Brown's handwriting, dated October 15, 1913, two years before Brown's death.

> *The idiots! Where did they get the idea that I was a war hero? When I found out what they were doing, it was too late to undo. I'd been away for six months only to return to find out they were erecting a statue in my honor. And then today, when they unveiled the plaque, I was stunned.*
>
> *Let this be my witness to the world: I hated the Civil War. I enlisted first on the Confederate side because their armies controlled this area. Then when the Rebs moved out and the Federals came in, I switched sides. I watched from my safe hideout on the mountain as the Blues and the Grays in the valley spilled their blood for an ideal. While they fought, I dreamed of an empire. War hero! I didn't even care who won. All I wanted to do was get on with my own life. I hate war.*

Hester breathed rapidly and heat suffused her body when she read the note for she knew she had finally learned why Brown's family had not been proud of him. How could one look up to a man who showed no loyalty to his country?

What would it do to Afterglow to learn that the man they revered had not lived up to their ideal? She could not publish this. The town's pride had already suffered enough during the past few weeks and she could not contribute added embarrassment.

When the snow melted, Kyle came back to Afterglow and Hester sent word to the boardinghouse that she wanted to see him. He soon arrived in jubilant spirits. "At last I'm breaking through that block of ice you call a heart," he said. "You've never invited me to see you before and you usually put me out when I do try to come in."

"Oh, be serious for once. I have something to tell you that I don't want others to hear." She took the Brown letter from a pigeonhole in the desk. "Although as a journalist it pains me to admit it, I've found something about your ancestor that I can't publish. You may want to destroy the paper. But at any rate, it's your decision now."

Kyle looked at her questioningly as he took the envelope. He scanned it, then read it more carefully and laughed.

"Don't you ever take anything seriously? Do you think it's funny that your ancestor was a coward?"

"I don't look at it that way. As far as I'm concerned this is the most intelligent thing I've heard that the old boy did. The Civil War was one of the most senseless incidents this country has ever experienced. If we would go to war now, do you think I'd rush off immediately, waving a flag? If he had fought in that conflict, he might have been killed, and I wouldn't even be here. Can you imagine the loss that would be to the world?"

"And to think that one reason I decided to suppress that information was to prevent you from being embarrassed!"

"I do appreciate it and I don't think the letter should be published, mostly because Afterglow's citizens would be distressed. But it doesn't matter to me."

"Does anything?"

"You do."

She ignored his remark. "You take the letter with you. I don't want to be responsible for it. After all, you brought it to me."

He tucked the envelope into his inner coat pocket. "I won't be here long this time. Our spring court circuit starts next week and I'll have a busy six weeks. But I wanted to check in and see how the celebration is coming along. And also to ask the mayor if he's decided to move."

"This is a laid-back town and they don't move fast on anything. Clint and I are the only ones who are making progress. The log raft ride is supposed to be the first of May and not one move has been made to bring in the logs or to plan the itinerary."

"Is the small town atmosphere getting on your nerves?"

"Most of the time I accept it, but I'll be happy to return home. Many times I've rued the day I agreed to come here."

"But if you hadn't, you wouldn't have had the pleasure of meeting me."

She gave him a scornful glance, and he exited with another laugh.

Although Hester was growing weary of Afterglow and its bickering, her eventual return to Detroit did not have much appeal. She would feel the absence of her mother more keenly when she returned to the familiar surroundings, and after today's letter from Molly, she knew she would not have her friend's company, either.

> *Dear Hester,*
> *I got married yesterday. That news is going to surprise you as much as it did me. I didn't suppose I would ever marry again, but I met Mario Salzabar soon after I came to my sister's. He's from Cuba, and has been living in the U. S. for about 10 years. He's a retired doctor, a most handsome*

*and distinguished gentleman. We will be living in
his modest home here in Florida.*

*Love,
Molly*

With a keen feeling of personal loss, Hester wrote Molly a
congratulatory note and enclosed a check for a wedding present. *Another tie of the past severed*, she thought.

Thinking of Molly's marriage turned Hester's thoughts to
Kyle. *Was he romantically interested in me or were his comments just more of his foolishness?* If so, she could not think
about it now. She also hoped he stayed away for she was
beginning to feel pressured with the amount of work to be
done, and she knew she could accomplish more with Kyle
Trent in Harrisburg. There was one advantage to her tight
schedule—she seldom gave any thought to her doubtful heritage and the elusive Toby she had hoped to find in Afterglow.

Even though Clint and Belle assured her that she was making great progress, she counted the swift passage of time by
observing the progress of the awakening forest. From her living room window she looked past the Byrd house and across
the river to a high mountain peak. The greening had started at
the river's edge and then had gradually moved up the mountainside. By mid-April she could see some green at the very
top and by that time the trees along the river were in full leaf.
When she observed a flock of robins tugging on recalcitrant
worms outside her apartment, Hester knew that spring had
arrived and that she had very little time to finish the history
manuscript, which Clint wanted for printing by the first of
August.

By now most of the citizens of Afterglow ignored Kyle's
suggestion that the town be moved, had lost interest in
Geraldine Ledman's lawsuit, and laughed when environmentalists talked about Brown's exploitation of the forest. The
melting snow on the mountains and long periods of rain had

flushed the river to its highest, and two log rafts, ready for the journey down the river, had been anchored where a boat dock had once been.

Hester refused to ride on one of the rafts, choosing rather to follow the expedition from the riverbank. She had talked to Mr. Byrd about the skill needed to manipulate one of the rafts and she had been convinced that no one now living in Afterglow had the expertise to supervise the operation.

"Chances are they'll wreck on the rapids between here and the county seat," Mr. Byrd said. "I declined the offer to ride with the town's dignitaries. Some of the mayor's ideas for this celebration are stupid."

Smiling at his remark, Hester said, "I'll bow to the wisdom of ninety-five years, Mr. Byrd. I'll walk."

"That won't be so pleasant, either," Miss Eliza said. "You'll be going over terrain a goat couldn't cross. Besides, Father, Charles Benson is going to pole one raft. He knows how it's done."

Hester still did not choose to ride on a raft, although Charlie Benson had earned her respect. He had made some beautiful replicas of the vases and curio shelves once manufactured by the old furniture factory. Several of the townspeople had met to clean out two rooms of the factory to make a place for Charlie and a few apprentices who wanted to learn the craft from him. They intended to have a good supply of souvenirs ready for the summer trade. And Hester was expecting many tourists, for some of the articles she had sent to her Detroit newspaper had been picked up by Associated Press and Afterglow's name was on the lips of people from coast to coast. She was grateful that she had some income from these articles, for she had received only a pittance of the grant money and if it had not been for the checks for her freelance work, she would have been forced to dip into her savings for everyday expenses. Even considering the low cost of living in Afterglow, she was going in the hole on this venture, and she often wondered why God had directed her steps in this direction.

One morning in late April when she was editing an interview she had had with Sadie, the restaurant owner, about the early eating places in Afterglow, a teenager who often ran errands for Clint brought a note to Hester.

> *Imperative that I see you right away.*
>
> *Clint*

Hester turned off her computer, put on a lightweight jacket, and headed downtown, grateful for a reprieve from her desk. The weather was so beautiful that it was difficult for her to stay inside. She was in Clint's office ten minutes after she received his note. He closed the door behind her.

"I receive issues of several out-of-town newspapers and this one from Harrisburg really gave me a jolt," he said as he handed her a newspaper and indicated an article on the inside section. The headline leaped off the paper toward her: *TOWN HONORS MAN WHO SHOWED THE WHITE FEATHER.*

She read the article aloud, her voice rising in volume with each word. " 'It isn't unusual for war heroes to be commemorated. Who hasn't heard of Andrew Jackson, William T. Sherman, Robert E. Lee? But there's only one town we know that has erected a monument in memory of someone, whom, to use a kind name, we will refer to as a conscientious objector.' "

There followed an unedited version of Brown's letter that Hester had given to Kyle. She felt blood rushing to her face, and her eyes blazed green when she looked at Clint. "Why did he have that published?"

"Then I take it, this comes as no surprise to you."

"To see it in the paper certainly surprises me. I found that letter in a packet of papers and pictures Kyle brought me. I gave it back to him and he agreed that it shouldn't be made public because of the impact it would have on Afterglow."

"This will put Mayor Stepp in the hospital."

"Maybe he won't see it."

"Don't count on it. This kind of news travels fast."

The telephone rang. After Clint answered, he listened silently for a few seconds, a crooked grin creasing his face.

"You're in luck," he said. "She happens to be right here."

He handed the telephone to Hester and with his lips formed the words, "Kyle Trent."

"Yes?" Hester spoke sharply into the mouthpiece.

"Why don't you install a telephone at your place? I've had a hard time contacting you."

"Because I don't want to be bothered with telephone calls."

"There's something in our local paper this morning that's going to make you unhappy." Hester held the receiver away from her ear and motioned for Clint to come closer and listen.

"I've already seen the paper here in the *Courier* office and you're right; I am unhappy."

"And I thought I could prepare you for the blow! I'll bet nothing has ever traveled that fast in Afterglow before. Well, I didn't do it."

"You had to. You had the paper and from the way I remember, it was printed verbatim."

"But I didn't. I've been busy since I returned to Harrisburg and I hadn't thought any more about my ancestor's letter. It was still in my coat pocket where I'd placed it at your apartment. I'm not the neatest housekeeper in the world and occasionally my sister comes in and sweeps out the place. She did that last week, and gathered up all of my winter suits and sent them to the cleaners for summer storage. Apparently someone at the cleaners found that note and passed it to a newspaper reporter. You won't believe me, I suppose, but I am sorry."

"I do believe it. I don't think even you would be so mean as to print that deliberately."

"Thanks for your confidence," he said ironically. "Gotta run. I'll see you in a few weeks."

Hester handed the phone back to Clint and he replaced it in the cradle. "What do we do now?"

"I'll go warn Mayor Stepp so he'll know about this before it becomes common knowledge. Then I might as well print it in the *Courier*."

"Try to assure the mayor that this is the kind of publicity needed if we're going to flood Afterglow with visitors this summer. There are hundreds of humdrum celebrations and festivals throughout this country. Nobody pays much attention when they're commonplace."

"You're probably right. Conflict commands more attention than peace."

"I'll stop by the furniture factory and tell Charlie Benson to speed up production of the souvenirs and to make a sign to advertise the factory as a tourist site. And why don't you print some "Handmade in Afterglow" stickers to put on the souvenirs?"

≈

Hester did not go to the next council meeting, but she heard Clint's account before reading about it in the *Courier*.

"If Afterglow isn't on the map after all of this, I'll be surprised," he said with a wide grin. "Some representatives from the American Legion Post in the county seat came to the meeting and demanded that we tear down Brown's statue. The mayor really has on his sword and shield now, and he's so angry because people are picking on his town that he's gone to war. He personally evicted the men from the council chamber."

Hester wrote up an account of Brown's memo and the council meeting results after Clint went home, and the next morning she left early to take it to the county seat to fax it to Detroit. The town of Afterglow still slumbered. As she passed Brown's statue, she braked suddenly—someone had painted a vivid white feather the length of the statue! Angrily, she reversed the car and headed toward the Noffsingers'. She pounded on the door until a sleepy Belle opened it.

"Hester! What's wrong?"

She pushed past Belle into the living room. "Someone has painted a white feather on Hezekiah Brown's statue! This has gone too far." Clint came yawning from the bedroom, wrapping a robe around him. "Should I telephone the mayor, Clint, and perhaps he can have the paint removed before anyone sees it?"

"I'll telephone him, but it's probably too late. It's pretty difficult to remove paint from stone. Why were you up so early?"

"Going to the county seat to fax an article to my newspaper."

"Go on. I'll notify the mayor. He's not so vulnerable as he once was. Nothing will surprise him now."

True to Hester's prediction, within a week the town's streets were crowded with curious tourists and reporters. Miss Eliza's boardinghouse and the motel were packed every night and the owner of the Grand Hotel talked of opening it up.

Belle had already rented part of the hotel for her craft show and when the women went in to clean it for the upcoming show, they helped refurbish rooms on the second floor for rental.

"The heating system doesn't work, but I can provide electric heaters if the weather is too cold," the owner assured Hester. So in the next article to her newspaper, Hester touted the novelty of staying in the old hotel.

> *The furnishings are reminiscent of the early 1900s. Don't expect a plush inn for the rooms are somewhat rustic, although they do have the amenities. But the view from the windows will keep you from noticing the lack of a telephone or television. Make Afterglow a part of your vacation schedule this year.*

On the day of the log raft ride, Hester, dressed in a sweat

shirt, jeans, and heavy boots and with a camera slung over her back, was ready to follow the rafts downstream as far as she could. Where the river narrowed between two high peaks, she would have to climb a mountain trail, but by now she had adjusted to the altitude and she intended to try it.

Kyle had returned from Harrisburg and without invitation had made known his intention to hike with her. When they reached the site of the old boat dock, a large group of tourists and natives were ready to follow the raft downriver and the bank was lined with interested spectators waiting to see the departure.

Clint and Ray were the rollers on the first raft. Ray had ridden a few rafts when he was a boy, but Clint admitted that he had never been on one before. The signal was given and the crew untied the raft and jumped aboard as the craft eased out into the current. A television cameraman rode on their raft, for Mayor Stepp was intent that the camera focus on the raft bearing the town officials.

Charlie Benson supervised the second raft and he suggested that the passengers sit down, but Mayor Stepp ignored his advice and continued to stand in full view of the camera and the spectators. When the raft was about ten feet from the bank, it tipped quickly, and before Benson could right the raft, Mayor Stepp and two councilmen tumbled into the shallow water. When the three men sputtered to a standing position, Benson helped them back onto the raft and they sat where he indicated.

"He did that deliberately," Kyle whispered. "He's too good at the job to have made a mistake. Look at the way he crosses those logs and directs the raft out into the current."

Benson was dressed in a red flannel shirt, loose overalls, and a red cap covered his curly hair. He moved as confidently as if he were on a solid floor rather than on a log raft as he maneuvered the rough craft toward the middle of the river.

"You're probably right and I doubt the mayor will give him

any more trouble. Mayor Stepp may think he's the star of this show but Benson is the one people will remember."

"And the preacher isn't doing too badly, either. Let's go," Kyle said. "We want to reach the rapids before they do. Should be some interesting photos from there."

They made slow progress walking along the river, for there was no trail and their way was obstructed by fallen logs, green briars, and other vegetation. They stopped trying to find an easy route, and plowed through the underbrush.

"We'll never make it," Hester complained.

"The rafts won't be going fast, either. We should make it to the rapids but we might as well forget about following them to the county seat. Once they hit the white water, they'll travel quickly."

One of the hikers had brought a machete, so he started cutting a path for the hikers, and although their clothing was tattered, their skins bruised and briar-scratched, the cavalcade of the curious did reach the rapids before the rafts did.

"But none too soon," Kyle said, pointing upstream. "There they are."

Hester stared at the gorge below them. The mountains narrowed at this point and as far as she could see, large boulders littered the streambed. White-capped water swirled around the rocks and she could not see any opening large enough for the rafts to pass through.

"And you actually suggested that buildings could be moved down this river on rafts!" Hester said sarcastically.

"At that time I'd never heard of this gorge and rapids," he defended himself. "They'll have to take the buildings by truck."

"Ha!"

When the rafts approached the rapids, Benson took the lead, and while the mayor and his dignitaries sat meekly, the bank robber's descendant took them safely through the first series of rapids. The spectators cheered the wet but safe rafters. Benson poled his raft into a protected spot and took up a foghorn to transmit information to the other rafters.

"It's not so bad, Reverend. More water than it appears," he called to Ray. "Hold to the left of that jagged boulder, keep your balance, and t'won't hurt to do a little praying. For when you start, you're going to come in a hurry."

Ray waved his hand indicating that he had heard the instructions. Hester felt sweat break out over her body and she leaned heavily on the walking stick she had picked up. She forgot to breathe, glad that Belle was not here to watch. Despite the life jackets they were wearing, instant death awaited anyone who was thrown against those huge boulders.

As far as Hester could tell, Ray did exactly as Benson had done, but when he reached the first white water, a bounding wave twisted the fragile raft and the sound of shifting logs was heard by those on shore. The cameraman was the first to topple into the water and when the raft finally reached the safety of smooth water, six of its passengers were floundering in the river.

Kyle and several other men rushed down to the water's edge to help the men to safety. With only a few bruises and cuts, they had little damage, except that the camera containing the documentary that Mayor Stepp wanted to air was lying at the bottom of the stream.

Benson and Ray agreed that the raft was damaged too much to continue the trip, so Benson and his passengers journeyed down river toward the county seat while the others tramped back toward Afterglow. By the time they returned home, a message had come from the county seat that the other raft had arrived safely, but Kyle and Hester were chagrined when they realized that in all of the excitement, they had forgotten to take any pictures.

❧

A few days after the raft trip, when Hester went to the furniture factory, she congratulated Charlie on his expertise in handling the raft.

"Old game with me, ma'am. Made my living in the timber industry for a long time."

"Certainly is too bad that your skill deserted you right there at the first."

"Well, accidents happen to the best of us," he said with an amused gleam in the eye. "Better for the mayor to have a little dunking than to cause all of us to wreck on the rapids."

"Did our tourists buy many souvenirs?"

"Just about cleaned us out. We'll have to work fast before we have that craft show."

"I know you're busy, but stop by the apartment sometime and see if you can figure out why the top of my desk won't roll. I'd like to buy it from Miss Eliza if the top can be fixed."

"I'll come around after work tonight."

Later that night, Hester cleared the desk off and he spent fifteen or twenty minutes tugging gently on the roll top.

"There's some kind of paper stuck in the left slide and that's holding it. I'll take it apart. We might jerk the papers out but that could damage the papers or the slide. Also, the papers might be of some worth. I'll see what I can do."

Hester brought him a cup of coffee and a tray of cookies. "At least have a snack before you start. You'll be late for your dinner."

"The old woman knows by now to cook for me when she sees me coming."

In an hour, Charlie had removed a packet of letters from the desk and had the roll top sliding up and down smoothly. The top letter was addressed to Tom Oliver Byrd, which did not surprise Hester for Miss Eliza's nephew had used the desk. After Charlie left, Hester ate a light meal for she was eager to take the letters to the Byrds and to offer to buy the desk. When she lifted the packet from the desk, the rubber band holding the letters snapped and they scattered on the floor.

Hester knelt to retrieve them and the first letter she picked up was addressed to Anna Taylor with a post office stamp of RETURN TO SENDER, on it. In the upper left-hand corner was written: *T. O. Byrd, Afterglow.*

With a thud, Hester settled down on the floor. Had she come to the end of her search at last?

eight

Hester's disbelief changed to shock. Surely she was dreaming! She had been in Afterglow for almost six months and she had scanned birth, death, and property records without finding a Toby, and the evidence she needed had been within her arm's reach all of the time. The Toby she sought was Tom Oliver Byrd, who signed his name T. O. By and sometimes lazily left out the periods. Why hadn't she tumbled onto that fact?

Her fingers trembled as she sorted through the packet. A few of the letters had been written to Tom by Miss Eliza when he was in the service, but six of the envelopes were of personal interest to Hester. Two of them had been sent to her mother at an address in Kentucky, which Hester recognized as her grandmother's address. The other four were letters that Anna Taylor had written to Tom Byrd. The letters from her mother were unsealed, so she read them first, and then she opened the ones that Tom had written to her mother. In a half hour she had the answer to the dilemma that had plagued her since December.

Tom Byrd and Anna Taylor had married after a whirlwind, week-long courtship when Anna was visiting her grandmother in Kentucky and Tom had been in basic training at Fort Campbell. He was sent to Korea immediately after their wedding and Anna had returned to her job in Detroit. Before she had gone to Kentucky she had broken her engagement to John Lawson, but as soon as she saw John again, she realized she still loved him and that her marriage to Tom Byrd had been a mistake.

John was willing to forgive her secret marriage and Anna wrote Tom a letter that she had started divorce proceedings. Then she realized she was pregnant. Within two months, Tom was back in the States, discharged from the service because of an injury he had received on the ship going overseas. A few months before Hester was born, the divorce was finalized and Anna took back her maiden name. One letter contained a copy of the final divorce decree.

So Tom Byrd is my father, not John Lawson! She laughed hysterically when it dawned on her that old Mr. Byrd was her great-grandfather and Miss Eliza was her great-aunt. Then her laughter gave way to anger—anger at her mother, at John Lawson, at Tom Byrd. Anger toward her mother and John Lawson because they had not told her the truth, and anger at Tom Byrd because he had apparently given his daughter away without any desire to see her again.

Now that she knew this, was she any better off? And what was she going to do about it? After a tense, sleepless night, she knew that she would do nothing. She intended to keep the letters written by Tom Byrd and her mother, for really they belonged to her more than to anyone else, and so she locked them in her traveling case.

After she nibbled on some toast and sipped a glass of milk, she went across the yard and found Miss Eliza in the kitchen, baking her daily portion of fresh bread.

"Guess what, Miss Eliza? I found out why the top of the desk wouldn't budge. Charlie Benson worked on it last night and he found the problem. These letters were wedged in the slide of the roll top."

Miss Eliza's hands were covered with flour, so she leaned over to peer at the letters. "Upon my word! Those are letters I wrote to Tom years ago. I'm surprised he kept them."

"Apparently your nephew was in the Korean War."

"No, the war was over by the time he was old enough to be

drafted, but they shipped him out for the army of occupation. He was involved in a nasty accident on the ship going over; an engine blew up and he was permanently injured. He was in the hospital for a few months before he came back here. That's when he lived in your little house. He wanted solitude."

No wonder I felt as if I had stepped back into time when I entered that building months ago.

"Does your nephew have a family?"

"No. He never married. He stayed with us for about a year, but he was restless for some reason. As soon as he recovered, he left and has never been back."

"So you don't know what he's done with himself?"

Eliza shook her head. "Maybe once a year I'll get a post-card from him and he's liable to be anywhere in the world. I don't believe he has a permanent residence. He's just a vagabond."

A great guy to have for a father!

"I'll lay the letters here on the edge of the table." Although Hester's desire for the desk had dimmed somewhat because she knew it had belonged to a father who had abandoned her, she said, "I wonder if I could persuade you to sell that desk to me. It's very versatile and I like it."

"Probably so. I'll give it some thought and decide how much I should ask for it." Miss Eliza kneaded the bread dough rhythmically. "What are your plans for the day?"

"This is the day they're going to start refurbishing the old covered bridge and I want to copy down all of those inscriptions before they're obliterated. I tried to tell the mayor those messages add character to the bridge, but he wasn't inclined to listen."

So people in Afterglow didn't know that Tom Byrd had been married, Hester thought as she went back to her house. And they wouldn't know after she left here, either. She had been born a Lawson and she would stay one.

On the way to the covered bridge, Hester met Ray and she

said, "If you aren't too busy, perhaps you could help me today."

"It will be a pleasure. What are you going to do?"

"Copy the inscriptions from the covered bridge before the workers destroy them."

"It's a good idea to record them, but they aren't going to be destroyed. The town council balked on the mayor last night. They told him the bridge could be repaired, but not painted inside. That's no way to preserve the history he's concerned about. Why, my own initials and my childhood love's are there! I carved them one midsummer night."

"Is that the girl you married?"

"No. I had dozens of heartthrobs after that. I met my wife when I lived away from Afterglow." A musing look crossed his face and Hester surmised he was recalling their time together. "We had a good marriage. I still miss her."

"Have you thought of remarriage?"

"Thought of it, yes, for a good wife is an asset to a minister, but I'm in no hurry. Do you want to be considered as a candidate for Wife Number Two?"

She laughed. "I wasn't hinting, but I can think of worse things. You've been a big help to me this year, but I don't have time to consider a proposal now."

They walked into the coolness of the covered bridge. "And what can I do to help you now?"

"Mostly keep me from being hit by a vehicle while I record all of this information."

Hester soon filled several sheets of yellow legal pad with notations of the type expected of teenagers such as hearts with arrows through them and bearing words like "Bob loves Susie." She found "Ray loves Bernice" and they laughed together about it.

"Ah, ha!" she cried. "Wonder if Belle has seen this? 'Clint loves Alta'."

"There's no problem if she has. Alta moved away from

Afterglow years ago and she's happily married in California."

Hester did not mention one inscription she found: "Tom loves Anna," and underneath in small letters, hardly legible, "but she doesn't love him."

"I believe we could use a new sign," Ray said, indicating the faded words painted on a square, warped board near the entry of the structure.

AFTERGLOW BRIDGE
ERECTED IN 1915

The board hung sideways and Hester tucked the notepad under her arm and attempted to straighten the sign. It swung slightly and slid down the side of the bridge, landing at Hester's feet. "Whoops! The nail that held it in place has rusted in two."

Ray waited until a car whizzed through the structure and then he joined her. "There's a drawing behind the sign."

"Looks like a map," Hester said, peering at the blurred markings.

"You may be right. If we can get rid of all that accumulated dust, we might tell what it is. I'll wet my handkerchief in the river and see if I can wash off the grime."

By the time Ray returned with the wet cloth, Hester had finished recording the other crude writings on the bridge. Ray rubbed lightly at the edge of the drawing. As the figures became plainer, he wiped more rapidly and a smile crossed his face.

"I suppose I'm a fool to even mention it, but this does seem to be a map of some kind and there are two initials down in the corner. Looks like *A. B.* Do you suppose this could be a map showing where Aaron Benson stashed the gold he took from the Afterglow bank? The story has always been that he buried the treasure before he left the region."

"Yes. Mr. Byrd told me that."

Hester and Ray looked alternately at one another and then quickly away for a good two minutes. Hester's thoughts whirled.

"I suppose we're thinking the same thing. Should we nail this sign back over the map and forget what we've seen? With everything else that's happened, all we need to completely ruin the centennial celebration is to have a treasure hunt in these mountains."

"It would be great publicity for Afterglow, though," Ray said thoughtfully. "I'm for telling it."

Hester waved her arms in resignation. "You'll have to live with the consequences. I'll be leaving in a few months."

"At least let's tell Clint and get his opinion."

"Replace the sign until you've had time to confer with him. I'll stay and keep guard while you go into town."

Hester walked back and forth across the bridge, dodging from side to side to miss the occasional vehicle that crossed. She thought about the pathetic note Tom Byrd had left behind. It seemed cruel of her mother to marry him and then desert him so soon. Hester had never had any ill feeling toward her mother and she did not like the fact that she felt this way now. If she could only see Tom Byrd, perhaps she would know why her mother had not chosen him. But on the other hand, she hoped she would never see him. It would be her luck to have him come back while she was here, but if he had already stayed away for almost thirty years, it was unlikely he would return until after the celebration in October.

In less than an hour, she heard a car coming from Afterglow at a rapid speed and Mayor Stepp brought his Buick to a sliding halt at the end of the bridge and ran toward her.

"Don't touch it! Don't touch it! This may be important historical data."

Hester lifted her hands high. "I'm not touching anything."

Clint and Ray hustled into the bridge and Clint and Mayor Stepp scrutinized the map.

"This must remain a secret until we can have someone interpret the map. Looks to me as if this arrow starts at the river and goes up on the western mountain about halfway, then comes down toward the river again where the route crosses to the Afterglow side."

Clint, in his quiet way, stared at the drawing a long time before he said anything, and then he cautioned, "Mayor, this may be nothing but a hoax. It could have been drawn in recent years and simulated to look old. My grandfather was always convinced that the Benson gang took the money with them. And Charlie says his ancestor left this country after that robbery and went to live in South America. That would have taken some money."

If the mayor heard Clint, he did not heed his warning. "We'll contact the university and see if they have an expert who can decipher the plan."

"The way I read it," Clint continued, "after the arrow swings around on the mountain, it crosses the river several miles below the bridge and cuts a figure *8* before it points to a rock. If that indicates the money was hidden under a rock, we wouldn't have to move more than a million or so on that slope to find the cache."

"Clint, you're too conservative. What do you know about treasure maps?" Mayor Stepp said.

"Not a thing."

"Well, then, stop giving me unsolicited advice. Cover that drawing and I'll halt repair work until we've had it analyzed. Not a word about this to anyone," the mayor warned as he hustled out of the bridge and into his car.

At least it is comforting to know that Mayor Stepp is not my father, Hester thought, the only good thing so far she could say about her discovery of the night before.

Before they nailed the board back over the drawing, Hester made an exact copy, or at least as closely as she could determine, of the map for the history book.

"I'm glad you're making a sketch of it," Ray said, "for if I were a betting man, I'd wager everybody in Afterglow will know about this before dark, and by morning, the drawing will be so smudged, no one could decipher it."

"I wouldn't bet with you on that," Clint laughingly said. "The outcome is too sure."

"I wonder if the mayor has considered who will claim this gold if it's found."

"Good question, Hester," Ray said. "I'd assume it would go to the bank of Afterglow, or to an insurance company if the bank had been reimbursed for the loss. But that long ago, many banks might not have been insured."

"How much money was taken from the bank?" Hester questioned.

"The amount has grown with each telling through the years," Clint said, "but I think they took a bag of gold worth about twenty-thousand dollars."

"No wonder the mayor is excited."

"But Kyle Trent may claim it, for the chances are that the gold is buried on his land," Ray said.

❧

Kyle had been out all day with representatives from the State Department of Natural Resources looking over the property he wanted to sell them, and Hester wondered if she should tell him about the map. But she had always heard that if you had news too good to keep, no one else would keep it quiet either, so she decided to say nothing. If the news spread, she would not be at fault. Already she wished she hadn't been curious about what was behind the dilapidated sign.

The next morning when she opened her door, Kyle called to her from the window. "Let's go look for the treasure, shall we?"

Her annoyance must have been obvious for he said, "Did you think that it could remain a secret in Afterglow?"

"No, I didn't, but the mayor did. Where did you hear it?"

"Miss Eliza told me at breakfast."

"Give me an hour and I'll meet you at the front steps."

Hester wrote a news story about the discovery and drew another facsimile of the map, which she would fax to Detroit. She had not intended to spread the news, but the mayor apparently had already done so for she was convinced that the leak had not come from Clint or Ray. She hurried into her car and drove off the driveway.

When she and Kyle arrived at the bridge, people swarmed over the area. She could not even find a place to park, so she said to Kyle, "I'm going on to the county seat and send a report of this to my newspaper, that is if I can cross the bridge. I'll stop here in the middle of the road so you can get out."

"There's a policeman directing traffic. I'll ride on to town with you, if you don't mind. I want to buy a metal detector."

"Then you're really serious about hunting for the bank loot?"

"Why not? I have to do something for entertainment and I can't meet with the Natural Resources people over a weekend, so it will help to pass the time if I'm wandering around over the mountains. Do you want to go with me?"

"No, thank you. Clint warned me of the danger of rattlesnakes on the mountain and I need that kind of warning only once. I'll watch from the sidelines."

She maneuvered the car at a snail's pace through the crowded bridge. So many people hovered around the map that the traffic was reduced to one way in that spot.

"I'll never get close enough to look at that map," Kyle lamented.

"No need to. If you look in the file lying on the back seat, you'll find a sketch of the map. Copy it if you like. I'm faxing the original to my newspaper."

Kyle studied the map while Hester traveled several miles. "This is a pretty simple map but I suppose a bank robber of a century ago wouldn't have been much of a cartographer. It seems to me that a person could save a lot of legwork if he would stay on the eastern side of the river and walk down the bank looking for the crossing spot. The way I read it, the route crosses the river near a clump of three spruce trees, and on the eastern bank the marker is a pile of rocks. All I need is to find that pile of rocks and go from there."

"Good luck!"

"What do you mean by that?"

"Think what floodwaters could have done to the rock pile. Also, that clump of trees would have changed somewhat since 1915. That's when the bank robbery occurred."

"Don't spoil my pleasure. This will be a fun way to spend the weekend."

While Hester used the fax machine in the post office, Kyle bought a metal detector and a shovel. When they neared Afterglow on the return trip, Hester asked, "Do you want to stop at the bridge?"

"No, I'll need to change into the rugged clothes I've been wearing the past week. And I'll snatch a bit of Miss Eliza's lunch, too."

"I'll walk back to the bridge with you when you're ready to go. After all, I want to be on hand if anyone finds a fortune."

When they arrived at the bridge, Charlie Benson was leaning against the bridge, an amused expression on his face.

"Why aren't you searching?" Hester asked him. "After all, your relative was involved."

"I've heard enough about Aaron Benson to know he never left any money behind, and I also understand he had an odd sense of humor."

As Kyle and Hester walked along the riverbank, Hester pondered Charlie's amusement and she remembered how he had dumped the mayor in the river. If this were a hoax, had Charlie perpetrated it? Hester considered him one of the most intelligent men she had encountered in Afterglow and she knew he was cunning enough to come up with the idea. But the sign appeared as if it had not been moved for a long time and Hester personally believed that Aaron Benson had drawn the map.

When Kyle determined he had found the correct pile of rocks and started climbing the mountain, Hester strolled back to the bridge, which was a beehive of activity. In addition to those wandering around on the hills with picks and shovels, dozens of the less active citizens lounged in the shade of trees and observed. Sadie, from the restaurant, demonstrated ingenuity, however, by peddling sandwiches and beverages from the back of her station wagon. She was doing a good business, too, for in addition to Afterglow's population, carloads of strangers crossed and recrossed the bridge.

Belle and Ina were among the spectators, and Belle signaled for Hester to join them on a blanket spread beneath a maple tree.

"Where's Clint?"

"At the *Courier* putting out a special edition. He hopes to have them here for sale in a couple of hours. He's reproduced the map and copied an account of the Benson robbery from an old newspaper. He's making a one-pager for a souvenir, but I know many people will buy it to use the map. This has been an exciting year."

Clint sent the first hundred copies of the special edition to the bridge by midafternoon and his employee sold them without leaving the car.

Mayor Stepp, wanting to be sure he was in on the discovery, had persuaded Ray to haul him around over the mountains on the four-wheeler, but Aaron Benson's sense of humor routed the trail over rock cliffs and other places where Ray could not take the vehicle. Too hefty to do any hiking, Mayor Stepp pouted when he had to give up the chase.

By nightfall, no treasure had been found for the map had led the searchers to many false clues.

"I'm going to hold the worship service down at the bridge in the morning," Ray informed Hester as they walked back toward town at dusk.

"I had been wondering what this would do to your morning worship."

"I'd have a sparse crowd because everyone is too excited. They want to be where the action is, so we'll gather down by the river."

"How will you pass the information to everyone?"

"You ask that after being in Afterglow for several months?" He smiled. "I'll telephone a few key parishioners and ask them to spread the word."

When she left him at the parsonage, Ray said, "I'll need to change my sermon though, so I won't have much sleep tonight."

Kyle came in soon after Hester reached her apartment and she laughed at his appearance. He had lost his cap and his blond hair was tangled with leaves and twigs. His clothes were torn in general and one long scratch spread down the side of his face.

"If that map doesn't take you on a wild-goose chase," he grumbled. "One place I had to climb a tree to see the next clue."

"Look on the bright side. You've had your exercise."

"And also missed my dinner. Miss Eliza eats at six o'clock sharp and at that time I was falling over a rock cliff. Want to come to the restaurant with me?"

"I'll prepare a sandwich for you and I have a gelatin salad. You can wash up in the bathroom."

"Make it two sandwiches. I'm starved. . .and thirsty, too."

Kyle did not stay long after he had eaten for he said, "I'm bushed. I'm going to bed so I can be out on the mountain again tomorrow." Evidently his strenuous day had not dulled his appetite for the search.

"Ray is going to have morning worship down by the bridge."

"I'll stay for that, and then start exploring again. You should come with me."

With a smile, she shook her head.

&

Hester and Kyle went to the bridge at ten o'clock in time for Ray's service. Ray stood behind a podium placed on a level spot near the bridge and a large congregation had spread out on the rough ground around him. Many people had brought their picnic baskets and coolers and a holiday feeling was in the air.

Ray's text from Matthew, Chapter 6 caught his hearers' attention immediately. " 'Lay not up for yourselves treasures upon earth. . .But lay up for yourselves treasures in heaven. . . For where your treasure is, there will your heart be also.' "

He used these words as a point of departure to indicate the futility of worshiping material possessions and to stress the importance of spiritual values. He used Jesus' parable from Matthew, Chapter 13: " 'Again, the kingdom of heaven is like unto treasure hid in a field; the which when a man hath found, he hideth, and for joy thereof goeth and selleth all that he hath, and buyeth that field.' "

As Ray compared the advantage of sacrificing earthly possessions for a place in God's kingdom, Hester wondered if the citizens of Afterglow held the proper appreciation for a man like Ray. They probably did not realize the treasure they had in him. Her thoughts turned to his offhand remark about Wife Number Two. Had he been serious? And how had a woman who had never considered marriage become involved with two eligible men? Perhaps that was the most noteworthy news of the summer!

By late Sunday afternoon, the trail had led the gold seekers to a knoll surrounded by a marsh, not far from the bridge. Kyle walked around the area and his metal detector transmitted positive signals. When Mayor Stepp heard that, he plunged across the swampy area, knee-deep in the mire. But he did not go alone, for soon a dozen men were digging at the spot where Kyle had received a reading.

From their vantage point near the bridge, Belle and Hester watched in fascination. The men talked excitedly, running from one spot to another to peer over the shoulders of those who were digging in the rocky ground.

"We've found it!" a man cried excitedly.

"Swamp or no swamp, I'm going over," Hester said, and she plunged into the marshy area that tugged at her shoes. By the time she reached the knoll, she was barefoot and wet to her knees, but she pushed her way into the midst of the crowd. A rusty metal box lay in a large hole.

"Don't touch it!" Mayor Stepp shouted. He motioned to a man with a video camera. "Take a picture right where it lies and then keep the camera going while we lift the box out and open it."

"I've had the camera going for the past two days and I'm not about to stop now," the man retorted.

"Gently, now," Mayor Stepp admonished as three men tugged on the dirt-encrusted box. When they placed it on the ground, Mayor Stepp knelt beside it and posed for the camera. The hinges on the box had rusted and the lid lifted easily to reveal a leather bag. The men hoisted it from the box, and with trembling fingers, Mayor Stepp untied the leather thongs. A look of consternation crossed his face when he looked inside, and one of the men peering over his shoulders, groaned and muttered, "The dirty scoundrel!"

He lifted the bag and dumped the contents on the ground. Dismay spread across the face of the treasure seekers when they realized they had searched two days for a bag of pebbles. A piece of mildewed paper fluttered to the ground when the stones were dumped. Clint picked it up and read aloud, "Tough luck, Afterglow! We took the money with us. Signed, Aaron Benson."

The searchers reacted in different ways. Some of them

threw down their shovels and cursed the day they had heard of Aaron Benson. Kyle laughed merrily, causing many of the sober-faced people to glare at him. Hester looked around for Charlie Benson, who stood in the background with a sardonic grin on his face. The video cameraman apparently was delighted with this turn of events, for he took close-ups of the disgruntled who were too weary to even notice what he was doing.

Hester crippled around on the rough terrain to take photos of the bogus treasure. Mayor Stepp slumped on the ground, a picture of dejection.

"Look on the bright side, Mayor. It's been an entertaining weekend," Hester said.

"Why does everything we do turn out to be a joke?" he moaned.

"Not everything. The arts and crafts show will be fine."

"No, it won't. Something will happen. If nothing else, Kyle Trent's lawsuit hanging over our heads will ruin it."

"Did I hear my name?" Kyle said, appearing beside them.

Mayor Stepp waved his arm angrily and refused to look at Kyle, who laughed and took Hester by the arm.

"Are you ready to leave? I'll help you through the mud."

"I came over by myself."

"Yes, but now you're minus a couple of shoes. Let's go."

When they passed Charlie Benson, Hester asked Kyle, "Do you think he planted that map and the rocks?"

"I'm glad you're suspicious of someone else besides me. Why not accept the incident at face value? I think Aaron Benson did it before he left here."

"But Charlie seemed so amused about it all."

"It amused me, too, but you can't accuse me of planting the evidence."

Hester was glad to reach dry land and she gladly accepted Clint's offer of a ride back to Miss Eliza's. Her slacks were wet to the knees, and abrasions on the bottom of her feet ached and burned. She was not in a very good humor with Aaron Benson.

nine

Belle's art and craft show was a success in spite of the controversy over the future of their town. The room was crowded with artisans, and a blacksmith and a cooper demonstrated their skills beneath tents set up on the sidewalk. The traffic jam was worse than during the two-day treasure hunt and Mayor Stepp walked the streets in a state of euphoria, smiling and shaking hands as if his next election were at stake.

Hester conducted tours through the renovated furniture factory and promoted the sale of the souvenirs that Charlie and his helpers had produced. After all their worrying and planning, the centennial celebration was leveling off now into a satisfying experience.

The next week Kyle received confirmation from the Department of Natural Resources that they would buy his land for a state park, but a sale price could not be agreed upon until they knew whether the town of Afterglow was going to relocate.

Kyle pressed the mayor and council members for a decision and when they refused to move, he instigated a suit to force them out. When he talked to Hester about it, she said resentfully, "I think you're being obstinate. It might be legal to make them move, but it certainly isn't ethical. It isn't the fault of any of these people that their ancestors didn't pay for the land. They're innocent victims. And by the way, what about Geraldine Ledman's suit against you?" she added sarcastically.

"She doesn't have a leg to stand on. There are no records to prove how much Hezekiah Brown received for the timber he sold. And as for the environmentalists who have been lambasting me, they can't do anything. I haven't cut any of their precious trees."

When she argued with Kyle that Afterglow was growing and that he should forget his claim, he said, "You prove to me that they own this land and I'll be the first to say 'Fare thee well,' but I want things done legally. I have a lawyer's mind."

"And a scoundrel's heart."

"Maybe! Give you a few more months and you'll join Mayor Stepp in his praise of Afterglow. A true daughter of his in spirit."

She looked at him angrily. She still had nightmares about Mayor Stepp being her father. By mid-August, Hester delivered her manuscript to Clint for printing and then she started organizing the drama. Her first concern was a place to present it. There was no time to construct an outdoor facility, so she suggested that the hotel ballroom be converted into a temporary theater. I. M. Thomas had sent a note giving the size of the backdrop and they had to make the stage fit that.

While she planned the drama, her mind fretted about Kyle's lawsuit. *If only there was some way to prove that Brown had donated the land to Afterglow.* She went back to the courthouse and searched for another day, but without results.

When she shared her concern with Ray, he said, "I've been praying for a sane way to resolve this argument. There's still a possibility that the church minutes might make some reference to property exchanges. I haven't read all of them."

"I scanned every page when researching for the history, but I'll go through the minutes again in case I missed something."

Hester spent the next week reading through the tedious church clerk's minutes, but still she found nothing that would alleviate the tense situation between Kyle and the town of Afterglow.

"You said you had a diary of Reverend Hartwell's, the

founder of the church. I don't suppose there are any clues in it."

"The diary I have deals with his year at Afterglow and the area was a company town long after that. I'd judge that Brown turned the property over to the town about 1910."

"That's the way Mr. Byrd remembers it." Hester stared out the window of Ray's office at the shimmering sunlight on the lazy river. "If Hartwell kept one diary, perhaps he would have had others. Where did you get the one you have?"

"From a descendant of the Hartwells who lives in the county seat. It hadn't occurred to me that she could have any papers relevant to a land deal, but it wouldn't hurt to ask her."

"Do you know the woman?"

"I've talked with her on the phone several times."

"Then let's contact her to learn if she has anything else. I doubt that the Hartwells would have lost interest in the town after they left. They might have kept in touch."

"I'll telephone the woman and set up an appointment to see her."

Ray contacted Hester that night to say he had an appointment for the next day and that they should leave immediately after noon.

☙

Iris Hambleton was a gracious, sixty-year-old widow who met them at the door with a smile and a warm welcome. She led them into a small living room filled with furniture of an earlier era.

In answer to their questions, she said, "I have quite a few items that belonged to Ivan and Thelma Hartwell and when you have the chapel car on permanent display, I will donate these things to the town of Afterglow. This huge house is too much for me and I'm planning to move into a retirement village in Florida within a few years."

She took them on a tour of the first floor, indicating items that had belonged to the Hartwells. In the dining room, she stopped before a miniature organ, sat on the stool, and played, "Amazing Grace."

"The Hartwells used this folding organ in the chapel car."

"It still has a good tone after all these years," Ray said.

She took out a few items of china from a walnut cupboard. "They used these, also." Mrs. Hambleton carefully lifted a large Bible from a drawer and handed it to Ray. "This was Ivan Hartwell's. You're welcome to use it on Centennial Sunday, if you like."

"I'd be delighted to do so," Ray said, as he turned the fragile leaves of the Bible.

"A few of their possessions are stored in an upstairs closet, but I haven't looked at them for years. Would you like to see those?"

"Yes, please," Hester said.

Ray and Hester followed their hostess upstairs and into a small bedroom, and she indicated two small boxes, which Ray lifted from the shelf.

"Careful for dust," Mrs. Hambleton cautioned. "I don't keep these rooms cleaned like I once did."

Ray placed the two boxes on the dresser. "May we look through these?" he asked.

"Certainly. Draw up some chairs near the dresser so you can be comfortable."

"I'll search through one box. You check the other," Ray suggested to Hester.

Hester's box contained old store accounts that the Hartwells had kept over the years. And while historically it was interesting to learn that at one time a dozen eggs could be purchased for five cents, that butter sold for ten cents a pound, and that a yard of calico cost twenty-five cents, it did little to solve the dilemma that Afterglow faced right now.

Ray had better luck, however, for he found another diary kept by Ivan Hartwell. "Ah, ha!" he said after he scanned the pages. Then he started reading aloud.

" 'August 10, 1915. Today I returned to Afterglow to participate in an historic event. Although a dreadful controversy has rocked the little village for months, resolution of the conflict between Hezekiah Brown and his accusers proves that the Gospel still has power to repair breaches. "And you, that were sometime alienated and enemies in your mind by wicked works, yet now hath he reconciled." Colossians 1:21.

" 'The controversy was occasioned when several landowners accused Mr. Brown of unfair dealings. When they threatened to sue him to recover their losses, he rescinded his promise to turn the town of Afterglow over to its citizens. A mayor and council had already been elected to receive title to the houses and land that had comprised a company town.

" 'I counseled with Brother Brown and the others and this morning under the sway of the Holy Spirit, I preached a powerful sermon on the text, "Therefore if thou bring thy gift to the altar, and there rememberest that thy brother hath ought against thee; Leave there thy gift before the altar, and go thy way; first be reconciled to thy brother, and then come and offer thy gift." Matthew 5:23-24.

" 'When I urged a cessation of the bickering, Brother Brown and those others involved came forward, shook hands, promising to end the strife. The landowners agreed to drop their suit against Brown and he pledged a speedy transfer of one hundred acres of valley land to the town of Afterglow.' "

Ray turned the page, but there were no more entries.

"That's what we're after," Hester said, "but is it legal enough to satisfy Kyle?"

Ray unfolded another paper he found in the back of the small journal. "If that isn't, this should be." And he handed Hester a deed to the town duly signed by Brown and witnessed, although apparently it had never been recorded.

"Is this a copy of the document or do you think it's the original deed?"

"I'd judge it's the original but I don't know why it would

be in Hartwell's possessions."

Ray turned to Mrs. Hambleton. "Did you know this was here?"

"No, but let's check the date of grandfather's death. He had a stroke and was bedfast several months before he died. It would be in the old Bible I showed you. Bring the diary and deed downstairs and we'll see what we can learn."

Eagerly, the three of them rushed downstairs and Iris turned quickly to the middle of the old Bible. After some calculation, Ray said, "Ivan Hartwell died three months after that deed was written. Since he's one of the witnesses, it's highly possible that he was given the document to record but he had the stroke before he could take care of it."

"But how could people in Afterglow have received deeds to their property without this being on record?" Hester puzzled.

"I have no idea," Ray said.

Mrs. Hambleton accompanied Ray and Hester to the bank where they made copies of the church records and the deed and watched as she locked the originals in her safety deposit box.

"Shouldn't we take the deed to the courthouse?" Mrs. Hambleton asked.

"The deed is more than seventy-five years old, so I don't know that it's still valid," Ray said. "We'll have to take this up with Kyle first and then go to the mayor. I think Kyle will be reasonable."

"Yes," Hester agreed, "he wants what's coming to him but he won't sanction anything illegal. I've found that he models his life on Christian principles."

As they drove back to Afterglow, congratulating themselves on the day's outcome, Ray said, "And, of course, this shoots holes in Geraldine Ledman's suit, also, and proves why the litigation papers she has were never finalized."

"I'm glad, for I don't think it's fair for Kyle to pay for his ancestor's faults."

"Is Kyle my competitor for the winning of your hand, Hester?"

She flushed and lifted a hand to her burning face. "See how you've flustered me. Imagine anyone competing for the hand of a thirty-year-old spinster."

"I am serious, Hester. I've learned to admire you greatly this year."

"That goes both ways. But let's solve Afterglow's problems before we tackle any of our own."

≈

When Hester and Ray returned to Afterglow, he said, "Our first move is to approach Kyle. If he's at Miss Eliza's, ask him to come to the church office after dinner."

"Why all the hush-hush?" Kyle asked when Hester sent word that she wanted him to go to Ray's office with her. "Are you trying to force me to marry you against my wishes?"

"No. It's something more important than that."

"You sure know how to hurt a guy!"

Hester's throat was dry and she talked little on their way to the church. How would Kyle react to their discovery? She admired the man and thought more about him than was good for her peace of mind, although she sometimes suspected that he had a ruthless streak. But she did not know him as well as she thought, for when Ray explained the result of their trip to the county seat and handed him a copy of the deed and the pages from Hartwell's diary, Kyle's laughter resounded throughout the empty church.

"We haven't told anyone else about this. We thought you should know first," Ray said.

"Do you mean you've withheld this information from the mayor to cause him another sleepless night? For shame."

"Are you going to contest it?" Hester asked.

"Do you think I'm a crook? You shouldn't have such a thought when I've been working for months to make a good impression on you. Although I can't imagine how the property in this town has been bought and sold without a legal deed, it took only one mistake somewhere along the line to cause this problem." He tapped the old deed. "This is proof enough for me, but it's high time this transaction is made legal. I'll have to give it some consideration but probably I should make a new deed."

A curious smile spread across Ray's face. "If I can convince Geraldine Ledman to drop her lawsuit, would you be adverse to having a reenactment of the settlement between Brown and the landowners in a church service? I'd use the same sermon that Hartwell did."

"Drama right down to the end, huh? I'm agreeable, but I doubt you can make much headway with Miss Ledman." He looked at Hester. "You think I have a mean streak. What about her? But she won't get a dime out of me, if I have to fight it to the Supreme Court." His blue eyes gleamed like cold steel. "It will cost me very little for I'll be my own lawyer, but she'll waste a lot in attorney fees."

So, he does have a contrary streak. But, on the other hand, he is ethical and honest.

"Will this block your sale of the Brown property to the state?" Ray asked.

"It shouldn't. They've agreed to buy but no price has been guaranteed because of the uncertainty about the ownership of Afterglow. They may want to relocate the town, but that will be up to them."

"If we plan this church service, will that be intruding on your drama, Hester?" Ray asked.

"No. I've sketched more scenes than I can possibly use, anyway. It sounds like a good idea to me."

"The town council is meeting tonight," Ray said. "Shall we go and break the good news?"

"Wonder if Clint could take a video of our announcement? I'm sure the mayor will want this on the news," Kyle said.

"Don't worry. He'll have it aired, one way or another," Hester said.

❧

When Hester, Kyle, and Ray entered the council room, a dead silence greeted them and hostile stares were directed in Kyle's direction.

"Mr. Trent," the mayor said at last, "we don't appreciate having you come here to badger us again. We've told you that we have no intention of moving this town and that your claims are completely erroneous."

"I couldn't agree with you more, Mayor," Kyle said.

"It's an outrage for you to even suggest that we move. We've had a glorious history for one hundred years and we can look forward to more, especially if the surrounding land becomes a state park. You're being greedy to demand this of us. It's completely illegal."

"I couldn't agree with you more, Mayor," Kyle repeated.

"We—" the mayor stopped in midsentence. "What did you say?"

"I said, 'I couldn't agree with you more.' We come bearing good news this time." Kyle waved his arm toward Ray. "Reverend?"

Ray went to stand beside Mayor Stepp. "We have found the record of Brown's land transfer, thanks to Hester's persistence. She was determined that there had to be some record that Afterglow's title was secure."

As Ray explained the nature of their day's findings, Kyle muttered to Hester, "Well, thanks a lot!"

She nudged him to silence.

When Ray handed the mayor a copy of the deed and Hartwell's diary entry, he said, "Mr. Trent recognizes the validity of these records and will not contest them."

"We no longer have a lawsuit facing us?" the mayor asked.

"That's right. There's no blot on the town's escutcheon," Kyle agreed.

The council members applauded. Mayor Stepp, unable for a few minutes to speak, took a handkerchief from his pocket and blew his nose loudly. Then he said grandly, "Then we have no more business to come before the council. We were discussing how to deal with a lawsuit. Meeting adjourned."

"We're intending to have a special service next Sunday to celebrate this turn of events. I trust you gentlemen will honor us with your presence," Ray invited.

&

The next day, Ray and Hester drove to the county seat again to see Geraldine Ledman. Ray was most diplomatic when he explained the situation to Geraldine, asking for her cooperation in renouncing the claims against Kyle and inviting her to participate in the church service. She heard him out and then with a faint smile, she said, "You're most persuasive, Reverend Stanford, but your eloquence was unnecessary. Though I hate to admit it, our charges are doomed to failure, anyway, because we haven't been able to find a reputable attorney to take our case. I can't speak for the others at this point, but I imagine they will drop the issue. I, for one, will attend the church service. I don't enjoy living with controversy, either."

As they left the Ledman house, Ray said, "Looks as though it will take a lot of planning to have the service ready in four days."

"I'll do what I can to help."

"I could use you to draft a dialogue between Kyle and Geraldine Ledman."

"I'll give it some thought tonight and then meet with you in the morning to draft the lines. I'm becoming adept at writing dialogue after all the trials and errors of that drama," Hester said with a laugh.

"You could assist me during Centennial Weekend, too. I'm to represent Reverend Hartwell and ride in the chapel car as it comes into Afterglow. I need someone to accompany me as Mrs. Hartwell. Will you do it?"

She darted a quick look in his direction. "Oh, Ray, I don't

know! Wouldn't it be too suggestive and cause a lot of speculation? I don't think it's a good idea."

"We could announce our engagement before the celebration and end the speculation about our intentions. I want to
marry you, Hester."

They traveled several miles while Hester thought of the
best way to answer him. He had mentioned marriage, but no
hint of love.

"Ray, you've been a great friend and I don't want to hurt
you, but I believe I would hurt you more if I marry you than if
I don't. I don't love you. I suppose that's the reason I haven't
married before this. I've not loved a man enough to want to
marry him and I don't want a man who doesn't love me."

He threw a startled glance in her direction. "But—"

"Wait," Hester said. "You think you must marry because a
minister needs a spouse. But you're still in love with your
first wife. If we did marry, we're both mature enough that we
would be congenial. But the marriage would be lacking
something. I believe that ultimately we would both be disappointed in the relationship."

They climbed the mountain and were headed toward
Afterglow before he answered. "Perhaps you're right, but I
am disappointed. I've pictured you in my life. . .and I like
that image."

Hester shook her head in refusal, but tears stung her eyelids. It had not been easy to turn Ray down.

૨

On Sunday morning, Kyle and Hester walked along with Mr.
Byrd and Miss Eliza toward the church. She still had trouble
remembering that these two people were her relatives. When
she left Afterglow in a few months, would she put away for-
ever the story of her heritage? Should she tell Miss Eliza? But
she could not do that. If Tom Byrd had wanted to conceal his
marriage from his family, it was not up to her to tell it. But
what if she were to someday have a family? Would it be fair

to hide her children's true heritage from them?

"Why such a frown?" Kyle inquired. "This is supposed to be a day of rejoicing. If anyone should be frowning, it should be me. I'm losing a hundred acres of land in this deal."

"That shouldn't make a pauper out of you. Is the state willing to buy the rest of the land, anyway?"

"Yes, and to allow Afterglow to stay where it is. The executives have decided that the town may do them more good than harm, especially with all of the publicity generated by the centennial. They're thinking of starting a new slogan. Instead of: 'Afterglow, the town where nothing happens,' they want to call it: 'Afterglow, the town where anything can happen.' "

Hester laughed. "Not a bad idea at that. Once you've sold the land then, are you going to cut all ties with the region?"

"I intend to reserve a few acres on the edge of the park."

"To live here?" Hester asked in surprise.

"No, but I've become rather fond of my ancestor this summer and I want to keep a few acres for nostalgic reasons. I may build a vacation home on it someday."

The strains of the pipe organ greeted them as Kyle and Hester joined the Byrds in the family pew, a place she could occupy by right of birth. It gave Hester a warm feeling to know that she was a part of Afterglow's heritage.

A singer set the tone for the meeting when her solo opened with the words, "I have returned to the God of my childhood." And after Ray's sermon, not only did Geraldine Ledman and Kyle go to the altar and shake hands, but several other townspeople also presented themselves as having their differences settled.

At the conclusion of the service, dinner was served in the fellowship room. Hester had to agree with Mayor Stepp as he said over and over, "This marks a new day for Afterglow."

ten

"But, Miss Hester, what props do you need to produce the drama? Our budget is strained," Mayor Stepp protested when Hester repeated her request for extra funds.

"You can pay for them out of the price of admission."

"But we had hoped to put that in the city treasury for other expenses."

"Then you can take the cost out of my share of the grant money. I won't put my name to a mediocre production. You should have realized this drama would cost some money. Besides, with all of the tourists we've had in Afterglow, surely you've had a boost in the town's coffers."

The mayor sighed wearily. "All right. What do you need?"

"I've already received the backdrop from I. M. Thomas and he charged nothing. I expected his fee to be in the thousands, so we've saved quite a lot of money there. We'll need a sound system, spotlights, and costumes. I've found out where those can be rented; all I need is your authorization."

The mayor grudgingly gave his consent, but because he was so tardy with it, Hester had only one week before the first rehearsal to accumulate what she needed for the drama.

❧

As Hester surveyed the motley crowd before her, she wondered if they would ever have a drama suitable for production in six weeks. Lacking funds to hire experienced actors and actresses, Hester had to rely upon the townspeople for her cast.

A temporary stage had been built in one corner of the ballroom, which left capacity for 200 rented chairs to seat the audience. Small cubicles off the ballroom, used as lounges in the hotel's heyday, made excellent dressing rooms.

Four performances were scheduled during the celebration weekend, which meant they could accommodate only 800 viewers, and Hester wondered if the audience might exceed that. She reached for a mike, and said, "Let me have your attention."

The roar of peoples' voices lowered to a hum, and Hester continued, "I've distributed copies of the script around the room, and although all of you won't have an individual copy, there are enough scripts for us to read and walk through the drama tonight. Those with speaking parts should take a copy of the script home with them and start studying their lines. As you can see, there are eight episodes in the drama."

Hester could not speak above the rustling paper as they flipped through the pages of the script, and she paused to give the people time to satisfy their curiosity about the drama. After a few minutes, she continued, "Clint will be handling the sound system to provide special effects as well as background music. And we hope our electric switches will handle the backdrop and the curtains at the proper time."

She turned to Charlie Benson, who had volunteered to handle the curtains. "Go ahead, Charlie."

From his stool behind the curtain, Charlie pulled a lever on the control system and the heavy, rented curtains divided to show the Thomas backdrop behind the stage. An excited twitter of voices indicated the citizens' pleasure at the scene before them and Belle said, "That surely looks like our valley."

"I'm amazed at how well Mr. Thomas re-created the valley. I sent him several photos for reference; he does have a great talent."

Huge trees covered the landscape almost to the river's edge. A red-tailed hawk perched on the naked branch of a dead tree, and the valley seemed to have been painted from the bird's viewpoint. The junglelike underbrush presented a primeval appearance but the river curving through the valley looked much as it did today. Deer and rabbits watered at the river's edge and a lone buffalo waddled along the bank. A hint of autumn was seen in the faint coloring of foliage.

"The river forms a focal point for all of the drama and the first scene portrays the area before European exploration. Where are our Indians?"

Six teenagers separated themselves from the audience and Hester instructed, "You'll enter from opposite sides of the stage, close to the backdrop, to give the appearance you've come from the river. Your music teacher at school has instructed you in the dance steps you're to perform. Make this a dramatic scene for you're worshiping the land. If Clint will start the music, we'll see how you do."

The three boys were embarrassed but they tried not to show it, and the girls giggled, but after several false starts, they did a fair rendition of an Indian dance, as their movements followed the rhythmic beat of drums sounding from the taped accompaniment. As the low tones of cane flutes and the shrill wail of bird-bone whistles infiltrated the room, the dancers shook gourds and tortoiseshell rattles in staccato thrusts.

Two braves entered, carrying a bear on a pole across their shoulders, and two women brought baskets of acorns and dried corn and laid them on the ground. The six dancers semicircled the produce with shuffling steps. The tempo of the dance increased and they swayed in rhythm to the music, lifting their hands toward the sky to worship the Creator.

"You'll do fine with some more practices," Hester praised them. The crowd applauded and the teenagers left the stage, exhibiting more confidence than they had at first.

"In our next episode, we see Hezekiah Brown on his first trip to the valley. Kyle Trent has agreed to play the role of his ancestor who moved to the mountains from Tidewater, Virginia, when he was a youth. Brown first entered this area as a trapper."

Kyle tiptoed onstage, hand above his eyes, peering intently from one direction to another and looking like a stereotyped explorer who expected an Indian to jump from behind every bush.

The rest of the cast tittered at his antics.

"Kyle!" Hester said crossly.

A surprised expression crossed his face. "You don't like my interpretation of the scene?"

"This isn't supposed to be a comedy."

"Let me try it again." He jumped off the stage and reentered, this time performing the scene as Hester had planned. Charlie flipped a switch and a glow of light surrounded Kyle.

"A beautiful site!" he exclaimed. And then turning as if facing the sunset, he continued, "What a great place for a settlement. The river is large enough to provide transportation. And look at the afterglow shining on that valley. I'm going to camp here where I have a broad view of the region."

He walked around surveying the area, caressing the large trees, and set up a tent near the river. With an exaggerated bow to the audience, he exited. The girls giggled and Hester ignored him.

"The narrator will convey the audience from Brown's arrival until the opening of hostilities of the War Between the States in this area, emphasizing how it interfered with Brown's plans.

"Episode Three centers around the battle of Afterglow. Most of you will be needed in this scene. Clint has taped the sound effect of a battle and you'll be running back and forth, moving weapons and caring for the wounded. We won't go through this scene tonight because the props haven't come yet. But you might give us a sample of the tape, Clint."

As the tape brought sounds of drums and bugles into the room, Hester could easily envision divisions of raw recruits moving in battle formation, drums sounding the march, flags waving, artillery rolling, heavily laden caissons plowing through the mud, with hoofbeats of a cavalry patrol moving on the flanks of the battle. Then it seemed as if a gun spoke across the narrow valley and another and another until the air above them spawned countless explosions. The whole region was filled with the roaring of weapons, the moaning of the wounded, and the neighing of injured horses.

"Do you understand what you must do?" Hester asked. "You're to pantomime what the sounds say to you. Think you can do it?"

"Sure, it said a lot to me. I was one of those groaning and screaming," a teenager said.

"Did the fight take place around the covered bridge?" Belle asked.

"No, there wasn't even a settlement here during the Civil War," Ray explained.

"I fear my knowledge of the war is skimpy," Belle persisted, "but why were they fighting if there wasn't anything here?"

"The Federals were trying to drive the Confederates east of the mountains, and they didn't want to go," Clint commented with a laugh. "Our local skirmish was an engagement between the enemies leading up to the battle of Droop Mountain in November of 1863, which pretty much insured Federal domination in our valley."

"Thanks for that quick history lesson," Hester said. "After the battle, the narrator will explain that Brown left the area for years, coming back as a wealthy man to start the timber industry in the late 1800s."

Hester became more encouraged as they read through their lines. Episode Four dealt with Brown's establishment of a company town and of the Irish and Italian immigrants who came to work on the railroad. Next came the Hartwells in their chapel car and the wood hicks protesting violently the advent of Christianity, but little children flocked to the Sunday school conducted by the Hartwells. Afterglow grew around the sawmill where many people could find work, but growth also brought the gamblers and the prostitutes. Scene Five closed with Brown turning the town's property over to the elected officials.

"Okay, where are our wood hicks?"

When the ten burly men came onstage, Hester explained, "You guys will have the responsibility of portraying the history of the lumber industry. Since it's a bit difficult to bring in the trains, the sawmills, the log rafts, and the like, I've planned for you men to present a day in the life of a wood hick by your conversation around the campfire. I've written a script, but please add your own comments as you go along. Some of you will be washing and mending your clothing, others will be sharpening saws and axes. This was your time of relaxation, but chores still had to be done."

The men sprawled on the platform.

"I wonder how many more of us will meet the same fate as poor old Joe. He thought he had a future, but a tree falls on him and he's gone."

"It's a poor way to make a living to my notion. I've had about all of the dirt, filth, body lice, and violence I can stand. Joe died doing an honest day's work, but Bill was killed in a street brawl last week."

"Both of them are lying up there on the mountain in unmarked graves, so I suppose it doesn't matter much which way they died."

"If you want to complain about something, what about the prices at the company store? My old woman says the groceries they have ain't fit to eat and my paycheck is gone before she ever buys all we need."

"Great! You've gotten the idea, men," Hester interrupted. "This scene will be one of our best."

When the men left the stage amid the good-natured ribbing of their neighbors, Hester glanced at her watch. Was the time going to be right? She planned for the drama to last a bit over one hour.

"Episode Seven features the opening of the Grand Hotel with a spectacular dance in the new ballroom and most of you will have to participate in it. That will mean a change of costumes, but we'll manage."

As the cast read the lines, Belle whispered, "I can see why you needed costumes. It's surely necessary for this scene. I can envision the women, whirling around the floor in their satin dresses with the narrow slit skirts, high-heeled shoes, and transparent stockings." A pleasant smile lit her ruddy face as she hummed softly to the tune of Beethoven's "Romanze," playing softly in the background.

"The last scene," Hester explained, "will be more narrative than action. I've asked several of you to represent prominent figures in Afterglow's history in the past fifty years. We'll have a doughboy of World War I make a presentation. Mr. Snead is going to do a monologue citing the effect the Great Depression had on the town. Afterglow's participation in the Second World War will be presented by one of that war's veterans. Finally, the decline of Afterglow and our hopes for the future will be pantomimed by two of our high school students representing the Spirit of Afterglow Past and the Spirit of Afterglow Future."

❧

After that first rehearsal, Hester felt emotionally drained and she accepted Kyle's invitation to stop at Sadie's restaurant for a snack. Clint and Belle were invited, too, but pleading the need to put Ina to bed, they went on home.

Wearily, Hester waited in the booth, while Kyle placed their order for pieces of pie and cups of tea. When he joined her, she said, "I would like your opinion on the drama and I don't want any foolishness, either."

"Yes, ma'am," he said and drew his hand across his face as if wiping away a smile. "The drama is all right but you surely have an inadequate cast, including yours truly. I doubt you can whip us into shape by the first of October."

"We can't afford to hire professionals so this is the best we can do. The citizens love the idea of participating in the drama. It's true they're inexperienced, but so am I. I've never written a drama before, nor have I directed one."

Sadie brought their food. As Hester sipped on the tea, she said, "I can't imagine why I ever took this assignment in Afterglow." She laughed mirthlessly. "I actually envisioned that this project could be in the class of Paul's Macedonian call. If it was, I've wondered more than once what God was about when He sent me here."

"If you'll remember, Paul didn't have smooth sailing when he went to Macedonia, either. He was jailed and beaten and often kicked out of their towns. So you can't expect any better treatment. But I believe this was your Macedonian call so you could meet me."

Hester did not answer him because Mayor Stepp bounded into the restaurant. "How did rehearsal go tonight, Miss Hester? Sorry I had to be absent."

"Slow, but that's to be expected on the first night. It will take much work to be ready by October."

"Care to join us for some pie, Mayor?" Kyle invited.

The mayor agreed and sat beside Kyle while they ate, commenting on the coming festivities. "It's been lots of work but it's paying off. I had a meeting with the park officials today and they're including Afterglow in their plans. They want to buy the Grand Hotel and set up park headquarters there. They intend to offer tours to the top of the mountain via steam-powered locomotives and these tours will originate in Afterglow."

"Do they contemplate reclaiming the original millsite and Brown's home?" Kyle wondered.

"That's included in the long-range plans."

"Then it looks as if your faith in the future has been rewarded. I'm happy for you," Hester said.

Although she had often despaired at the mayor's pomposity,

she did believe the man was sincere in his desire to make Afterglow successful. But tonight she was too tired to listen to one of his speeches, so she looked at her watch and said, "It's about time for Sadie to close, gentlemen. We should leave."

As Kyle and Hester walked toward their quarters, Kyle said, "Let's take a drive. The night's still young."

"I'm willing. I'm too keyed up to sleep, anyway."

Kyle turned on the CD player when they settled into his Mercedes and Hester leaned her head against the seat as they drove in silence through the covered bridge and up the mountainside. Kyle parked at the turnout and he took her hand as they walked to the overlook. A full harvest moon bathed the valley in subdued light and the lights of Afterglow seemed dull in comparison.

Hester leaned on the stone wall at the edge of the precipice and breathed in the beauty of the night. "I'm glad I've finally gotten over my fear of heights. Now that I have, it's almost time for me to leave here."

"I understand why my ancestor liked this area. The view by night is as fantastic as at sunset. Seeing this I'll be able to give a better interpretation of Hezekiah Brown."

"Oh, you do a great job and you know it."

"Every attorney has to have some acting ability, I suppose. I've been doing a lot of acting this summer."

Thinking that he must have some meaning behind the words, she looked at him questioningly.

"Don't you have any idea that I'm in love with you?" he asked.

Hester's amazed look was the only answer she gave, but the sudden pounding of her heart indicated that his words were welcome.

He laughed lowly. "That's what I thought. All of these little hints and my innuendoes have been wasted on you. Why else do you think I've spent week after week in Afterglow this summer, thereby driving my secretary crazy because my law business is going down the drain?"

"Why, I supposed you were here on business with the park's commission!"

"That didn't take long. No, I've stayed underfoot trying to find the right way to ask a woman who doesn't even know I exist to marry me. Will you?"

"Will I what?"

"Marry me."

Hester moved away from the wall and eased her trembling legs by sitting on a nearby concrete bench. "I sound like the heroine in a melodrama, but this is so sudden."

"Why haven't you married before, Hester? You're personable enough and you have both beauty and brains, a hard combination to find these days. Are you in love with someone else?"

She shook her head in answer to his question. "I haven't been interested in marriage. I finished college and had just started a new job when my mother became ill and I looked after her for five years. During that time, my social life was curtailed."

"Why have you put up an invisible wall around you that says to males, 'Keep out'?"

"I don't think I have. And you're as old as I am. Why haven't you married?"

"I hadn't found Miss Right until now. Will you marry me?"

"You surely don't expect me to give you an answer now, when ten minutes ago I hadn't considered marrying anyone, especially you. I'm not sure we would be compatible, anyway. It seems to me that you go out of your way to annoy me."

"That's my nature. But mostly I did that as a defense mechanism so I wouldn't be too hurt if you turned me down."

She stood up. "Most of the time I never know if you're serious or not. If I should say I'd marry you, you're apt to say it was all a joke. Let's go back to town."

Kyle pulled her roughly into his arms and his lips stifled

Hester's startled gasp. Hester had been kissed often when she was in college, but never like this, and when he released her, she sank to the bench again, her breathing difficult, her pulse racing.

Kyle looked down at her and the moonlight revealed his face and eyes. . .eyes that gleamed with a tenderness that Hester had not seen there before.

"Does that convince you that I'm not joking?"

She nodded and released his gaze. Kyle took Hester's hand, pulled her upward, and with his arm around her, steered her back to his car.

"When will you give me an answer?" he asked.

"Not until this celebration is over, and I wish you had waited until then to speak. I already have enough on my mind."

"Just forget I've said anything. We'll start over later."

"That's easier said than done."

When they parted at the steps of her apartment, Kyle said, "I forgot to tell you Miss Eliza's important news. Her nephew is coming for the celebration."

That comment wiped out the excitement of Kyle's proposal and she was glad her face was shadowed so he could not see it.

"Which one?" Hester said harshly.

"I didn't know she had more than one, but this is Tom, the nephew who lived with her and who's been gone for years. She'll tell you all about it tomorrow."

"I can hardly wait," Hester said through lips that were so stiff she could barely open them.

eleven

Hester slammed the door behind her and hurried into the bedroom. Jerking clothes off the hangers, she reached under the bed and pulled out her luggage. She would leave tonight. Mayor Stepp could find someone else to direct his drama. She had done all the hard work. She would not stay here and face Tom Byrd. Why did he have to return to Afterglow now?

Dizziness swept over Hester and she eased down on the bed, praying for strength to still the hammering of her heart and the trembling of her body. Wearily, she pushed the luggage back under the bed and replaced her clothes on the hangers.

She could not leave. She had never run out on an assignment before and she could not afford to work for nine months without pay. Bitterly, she thought of the contract she had forced Mayor Stepp to sign. She had received only a meager advance for her work, and if she did not stay through the centennial, she would not derive any further compensation from her hard work in Afterglow. Could it be possible that Tom Byrd would not associate her with Anna Taylor Lawson? He probably did not even know what Anna had named her, and if he did not know she was from Detroit, he might not make any connection between Hester Lawson and Anna Lawson. She looked more like her maternal grandmother than she did her mother, anyway. She would avoid the man; that's all she could do.

As for Kyle's proposal, that would have to wait. She had always thought that one would know Mr. Right the moment you saw him, that there would be magnetic vibrations from one to the other. Although he had aggravated her, she had been interested in Kyle from the first. But could it be love?

They had shared some good experiences this summer and they had similar cultural backgrounds. But was that enough? Did love strike like a bolt of lightning or did it sometimes develop slowly?

❧

The next morning, Miss Eliza was on the back porch, shaking the dust mop, when Hester started downtown. Hester walked slowly toward her when she called, "Tom's coming home," her voice ringing with happiness. "I had a note from him yesterday. Seems he's read about the celebration in the newspapers and he wants to be here."

So my own scrupulous coverage of the centennial in the Detroit paper may have been the cause of this visit! But Hester could not help wonder if this was the way it was supposed to be. Was this God's way of directing her path this year?

"Where was he when he wrote to you?"

"The card was postmarked Chicago. He didn't say when he would arrive or how long he would stay."

"I'm happy for you," Hester said as she continued on her way. And that was true, but she just wished Tom Oliver Byrd, alias T O By, had waited a few more months to return to Afterglow.

❧

That night the commission met and finalized plans for the centennial weekend. A parade would start the festivities on Thursday, with the first presentation of the drama that same night. Following the drama, the centennial commission would host a reception for guests and locals. The mock bank robbery would take place on Friday, and on Saturday the chapel car would pull into its permanent home, with a worship service and dedication scheduled for Sunday.

Hester was so busy with the rehearsal every night, helping Clint distribute the histories, and working with Charlie Benson to prepare the factory for visitors that she easily pushed Kyle's proposal and Tom Byrd's arrival to the back of her mind during working hours. But they always confronted her at night when she tried to sleep, and each morning she was left listless without any decision in dealing with either Kyle or her natural father.

One of the aspects of a future with Kyle that concerned her was the depth of his Christian commitment. She had not observed any moral or ethical flaws in his character, unless one considered his obstinacy in the conflict with the town fathers over his ownership of Afterglow, but once he was presented with legal proof, he had yielded graciously enough. And he did attend worship services, but she wanted more in a husband than just a casual churchgoer.

"Lord," she prayed, "give me a sign about this man so I won't make a mistake as my mother did."

The Noffsingers and Hester collaborated on a float for the parade by making a huge plywood facsimile of the history book and decorating it with the words: A HUNDRED YEARS OF HISTORY. Clint intended to pull the exhibit with his four-wheeler, while Belle and Hester rode on the float and passed out brochures advertising the history books.

Kyle made a week's emergency trip back to Harrisburg concerning a case he was trying, and although he was missed in the rehearsal since he was the main speaking character, Hester was glad to be rid of his disturbing influence for a few days. With her thinking about both Tom Byrd and Kyle, her sleeping time was turning into nightmares. *Macedonian call, ha!* she thought more than once in the dark hours of the night when she yearned for sleep.

On the day of the parade, the weather favored them with a bright sun and wispy white clouds being wafted across the mountaintops by a gentle breeze. Despite her worry over the drama's opening, Hester enjoyed riding the entire length of the town and back, a course planned to make the parade a little longer. It was reported that every motel and hotel room in the county seat were sold out for the weekend and that there wasn't a room to be had in Afterglow, in spite of the fact that every household with a spare room had turned into a bed-and-breakfast. Even the mayor had laid aside his dignity and made one of the bedrooms in his spacious house available to a couple of teenagers, who in one day had raised the ire of the mayor's elderly housekeeper by their slovenly ways.

That evening, when Kyle escorted Hester to the rear entrance of the hotel, people were standing in line for two blocks, waiting to buy tickets for the drama. He squeezed her hand when he left her to go to the men's dressing room. "It's going to be great, so don't fret," he said.

Hester made last-minute checks to be sure all the participants were in place. They tested the sound system, which worked well. The drama was scheduled to begin at seven o'clock and fifteen minutes before that, Clint started playing soft music and the audience quieted in anticipation.

On schedule, Charlie opened the curtain and the six Native Americans slipped onstage in their buckskin garments. Watching from the wings, Hester marveled at the skill they exhibited after six weeks of practice. The audience exploded into applause more than once during their rhythmic interpretation of the Native American music that Clint played.

In the second episode, Kyle strode onstage, dressed in the fringed buckskins of a hunter. He led two mastiffs that had given him lots of trouble during rehearsals, but Kyle had a firm grip on them and they sat at his feet while he delivered his lines in a ringing voice.

Why, I really do love that man! Hester thought in surprise as her heart leaped in amazement. *With all the pressure on me, why did I have to realize that tonight?* But she had asked God for a sign, and she intended to wait for it.

When the curtain fell on the final scene, Hester wiped her perspiring hands on a tissue and breathed deeply. The repeated curtain calls assured her that the drama had been successful. Then Mayor Stepp took the stage and Hester groaned to Clint, "We can't have a speech from him. It's time for the reception."

With much gesturing and clearing of his throat, Mayor Stepp said, "We want to extend a special thank you tonight to the person who has done the most to make our centennial celebration a success. Miss Hester Lawson answered our Macedonian call for help and has kept our town from dying by bringing out the best we have to offer. Come out and take a bow, Hester."

The insufferable man, Hester thought, but with the best grace she could muster, she went onstage and received a standing ovation from the audience, while the mayor awkwardly, but discreetly, pinned an orchid on her dress, sticking her shoulder in the process.

A caterer from the county seat had been commissioned to provide refreshments for the reception in the main lobby of the hotel. Hester stood in line with Mayor Stepp and the centennial commission, while the costumed cast mingled with the guests. The place was so crowded that Clint echoed Hester's thoughts when he whispered, "I hope nobody shouts 'fire'."

Gradually, all the faces began to look alike and at first Hester did not recognize the casually dressed man with white hair and whiskers and intense gray eyes, approaching her with a smile on his face. After all, she had not seen him for eight years!

She gasped and said, "Why, Mr. Thomas! Can it be you? Why didn't you let me know you were here so we could have given you a public thank you for your work on the backdrop?"

"I didn't need to be thanked, Miss Lawson; that's the

reason I sneaked into town. We can talk later. I mustn't hold up the line."

He shook hands with Clint and passed on quickly.

"I want you to know," Hester said breathlessly, "that you just shook the hand of I. M. Thomas, the famous artist who contributed the backdrop for our drama."

"I thought I'd seen that guy before, but I hadn't heard of Thomas until you mentioned him."

"He's been on TV specials a few times. You might have seen him there."

Hester turned to smile at the next well-wisher. Her hand was numb by the time the last person in line passed her. She looked up gratefully when Kyle thrust a cup of punch into her hand.

"Come and sit down," he said as she drained the cup. "You've done your duty for the night. Belle and I have commandeered a bench so you and Clint can rest. I'll show you where it is and bring you some food."

"I'm not in the habit of having someone look out for me, but it seems rather nice. You were great in the drama tonight."

"I'm willing to take on a lifetime job of looking after you if you'll say the word," he whispered in her ear.

She smiled at him with a promise radiating from her eyes, but she could not give him an answer here. Hester eased down on the bench beside Belle and Clint, who held a chattering Ina on his lap.

"Do you suppose I'll shock anyone if I take off my shoes? I'm bushed," Hester said.

"Oh, you can do no wrong tonight," Clint said. "You're the popular one, but enjoy it while you can. You know how quickly Afterglow can change its loyalties."

Before she could unbuckle her shoe straps, Miss Eliza approached with I. M. Thomas by her side. She said, "Folks, I want you to meet the prodigal son. This is my nephew,

Tommy Byrd. You probably remember him, Clint, but the women wouldn't."

Hester half-rose from the bench and gasped. Kyle stepped to her side, but she waved him away.

Clint shifted Ina to his left arm and rose quickly to grasp Thomas's hand. "I thought you looked familiar, but I surely didn't connect Tommy Byrd and I. M. Thomas."

"That's a pseudonym I coined when I started out as an artist. I didn't know whether my work would be successful and I didn't want to put my real name to it," the artist said jovially, with a glance in Hester's direction.

"Oh, I get it," Clint said. "You simply used, 'I am Thomas.' Clever!"

The same way he'd turned Thomas Oliver Byrd into T O By, Hester thought bitterly. All these years when she had admired the work of I. M. Thomas, he had been Tommy Byrd. And not just Tommy Byrd, but her own father. Did he know? Had he known all along?

Hester sat her plate and cup on the floor. "Excuse me," she said. Miss Eliza looked at her in surprise as she rushed away, but she did not care if she was rude. She could not tolerate this news. All these months when she had thought her natural father was a ne'er-do-well, he had been a man of fame and fortune. Thankfully, this reception was not her responsibility and someone else could lock up the place tonight.

Hester walked to the apartment, changed into a sweater, jeans, and tennis shoes and walked the streets of Afterglow for hours, dodging anyone who looked as if they wanted to chat. She did not want to be at home when Miss Eliza and Tom Byrd returned. She could not face Kyle nor the Noffsingers. They must have been shocked at her reaction to Miss Eliza's nephew. But the most disturbing question facing her was: *Does Tom Byrd know who I am?*

It was past midnight before she went back to her apartment and by that time the lights were out in the boardinghouse.

She dreaded having to face her friends in the morning, because she could imagine their consternation about her behavior, but at least she could put off their questions for a few hours.

As it turned out, however, the next day brought so much excitement that no one even thought to ask Hester why meeting Tommy Byrd had been a shock to her.

❧

A loud blast awakened Hester and she stirred groggily. The little house vibrated and she wondered momentarily if there had been an earthquake. She peered at her alarm clock and decided to get up, even though it was only six o'clock. Her body and mind were as weary as if she had not slept at all.

The mock bank robbery was not scheduled until ten o'clock, and although she did not have anything to do with the reenactment, she did not want to miss it. She put some water on the stove to heat for coffee and she headed toward the shower.

"Hester," Kyle called, and she tied her robe and opened the door a crack. His blue eyes sparkled with excitement.

"The day has started off with a bang! Did you hear it?"

"Yes, what happened?"

"The bank has been robbed."

"Already? That wasn't supposed to start until ten o'clock."

"But this robbery wasn't on the schedule!"

"Do you mean the bank has actually been robbed?"

"Right. Clint telephoned me at the boardinghouse and wanted me to tell you. Let's hurry down there."

Hester dashed into the bedroom and donned sweats and a jacket in short order, and in a matter of minutes, they were jogging down the street. Kyle chuckled. "Nothing like a robbery to spice up the celebration."

Clint and Ray were in the crowd gathered around the front of the bank, which had been roped off by the police, when

Kyle and Hester joined them.

"What's the story?" Hester asked, her reporter's antenna extended.

"We can't learn much," Ray said, "but apparently some robbers got into the bank and used explosives to blow open the vault. The money and the robbers were gone when the police arrived."

A siren sounded and a police car stopped at the edge of the crowd. A deputy pushed his way through the crowd and into the bank. His voice carried to the waiting crowd. "Nobody has crossed the bridge since this explosion, so that means they're still in town."

"Or up on the mountain," Ray said, glancing around him.

"How do they know no one has crossed the bridge?" Hester asked.

"Some men have been working at the bridge's entrance most of the night to repair a rail at the crossing," Clint said. "It was damaged in yesterday's traffic."

"Of course, there's always the possibility of crossing the river by boat," Ray suggested.

A possibility the chief of police must have recognized, for he came out on the steps of the bank and called, "Folks, this is an emergency and I'm calling for citizen volunteers. A large amount of money has been taken from the bank and the thieves can't have been gone more than a half hour. I need men to patrol the riverbank and I want volunteers to comb the mountains on both sides of the river."

As the men raised their hands and shouted their readiness to help, Hester noticed Charlie Benson, standing to one side. Was it a smirk or a smile on his face? Hester wandered toward him.

"Aren't you going to volunteer?"

"Doubt they'd want me, ma'am. I'll probably be arrested for doing the job."

"Did you?"

"No, I didn't, but I might have, if I'd thought of it. This is more sensational than a mock bank robbery."

He drifted away and Hester joined Kyle, who had been assigned to patrol downriver. She walked with him along the river's edge. "Who do you think did it?" she asked.

"With all the strangers we've had in town, it could have been anyone," Kyle answered. "In my judgment, it was an amateur job because professionals wouldn't have used dynamite. There are more sophisticated ways to open a bank vault now."

"And I doubt this bank kept enough money to make it interesting to big-time bank robbers."

"The merchants have taken in a lot of money the past few days, but you're right, no astronomical amounts."

When they reached the bridge, Hester said, "I'm going back and keep an eye on what goes on in town. Be careful."

"Is that a maternal or a wifely interest?"

She ignored his remark and turned back. If she married him, she would have to put up with his particular brand of humor, but she could think of worse characteristics in a life partner.

A roadblock had been set up at the entrance of the covered bridge and it was not likely that any suspect could go through, but considering how easily packets of bills could be hidden in clothing, Hester thought they would need to frisk everyone. When Aaron Benson and his gang had made off with a sack of gold, it would have been more difficult to hide and to transport. Hester did not tarry at the roadblock for the sheriff's deputy eyed her suspiciously.

When she entered the city hall to find out the fate of the planned centennial activities, Mayor Stepp told her the mock bank robbery had been canceled, and he was inconsolable. Hester tried to reason with him, "You wanted publicity. This will direct much more attention toward Afterglow than a make-believe attempt."

"But I don't like to have my plans disrupted."

Hoping to be ahead of out-of-town reporters, Hester went into the *Courier's* office. Clint was trying to use the computer while holding the phone under his chin. When he hurriedly replaced the receiver, she asked, "May I use your phone for a few minutes to call Detroit?"

"Sure. Talk on it all day as far as I'm concerned. That will keep anyone from calling me. I have to finish this article for we must start the presses in a half hour."

When she had her editor/boss on the line, Hester said, "Since you've done a series of articles on Afterglow's celebration, you won't want to miss this one, and I want you to headline the story: AFTERGLOW, THE TOWN WHERE NOTHING HAPPENS."

She gave him a brief description of the robbery, as well as the parade and the drama's opening night.

"Is your work nearly finished there? When will you be returning to work?" her boss asked.

"By the middle of November, I'm sure. A few more days should finish my assignment here, but I'll need some time to readjust from Afterglow to Detroit. It's been a frustrating time."

After Hester replaced the phone, she said to Clint, "Is there anything I can to do help you? Remember, I've worked in a newspaper office."

"Yes. Edit and revise this article and do anything else around here that needs attention. I'm as bad as Mayor Stepp, so unnerved, I can't even spell correctly."

"C-o-r-r-e-c-t-l-y," she said saucily.

"Oh, cut it out. Get busy and earn your money."

She laughed at him and picked up the article he wanted her to edit. When she checked his article about the drama and reception, Hester noted his comment: *The most prominent guest at the reception was the well-known artist, I. M. Thomas, better known locally as Tommy Byrd. Afterglow welcomes home its long-lost son.*

After she edited the article, Hester answered the phone and fielded questions from those who wanted information, all the while thinking of her own problems. Would the drama be showing tonight or would the actors be on posse duty? When should she leave Afterglow to return home? Could she avoid Tom Byrd? Should she marry Kyle Trent? For the past nine months her whole life had revolved around a series of questions.

Considering the quiet life she had led in Detroit, she wondered why she had ever gotten caught up in this turmoil. Could she ever enjoy peace and quiet again? But if she married Kyle, she doubted that her life would be boring.

In the late afternoon, Belle telephoned. "They've found the robbers," she said excitedly. "The two teenagers who rented a room in Mayor Stepp's house. They were in the restaurant and Sadie overheard enough of their conversation to make her suspicious. A policeman came in about that time and he searched the pair, finding that they had most of the money on them. The rest was found in their luggage at Mayor Stepp's."

"But who are they?" Hester finally found an opening to ask.

"A couple of hoodlums from the county seat."

Hester quickly relayed the message to Clint before she rushed out on the street. Gunshots sounded all over the valley to recall the searchers. Dozens of irate citizens surrounded the police car when the two robbers were handcuffed and taken to the small jail in back of the mayor's office.

"The show must go on," Mayor Stepp shouted over the public address system that had been set up for the mock robbery's enactment. "Afterglow might be slowed down but never defeated. Drama tonight as scheduled."

Hester dashed back into the newspaper office to telephone this breaking conclusion to her newspaper before returning to her house. She met Kyle on the sidewalk in front of the boardinghouse. "Just look at me," he said. His clothes were covered with brown burrs and briers had torn his jacket and made a long scratch on his chin. "And after all this misery of climbing through the jungle, I didn't even catch the robbers."

Hester laughed at him. "Quit complaining. You sound like the mayor. I'll help you pick off the burrs, but we'll have to hurry. The drama starts on schedule."

"Forget the burrs. I'm going to throw my pants and socks away. I wouldn't consider cleaning these things. But who were the robbers? I assume they've been apprehended."

"A couple of teenagers, and from all appearances, they haven't been long on the road to crime. They looked scared to death when the police handcuffed them and took them to jail."

A look of concern crossed Kyle's face and he glanced down at his clothes.

"How long do we have before the drama begins?"

"About two hours."

"I'll have to go see those boys, but I can't go looking like this. If I hurry with a shower, I can talk with them and still be on time for the drama."

Hester laughed. "Why would you want to see them? Surely you aren't so hard up for clients that you need to solicit them in Afterglow."

He favored her with a disgusted look and headed toward the house.

"May I come with you? Perhaps I can do a feature story for Clint and for my paper."

"Be ready in a half hour."

❧

The jail consisted of two cells and a small anteroom where a bailiff stayed when anyone was housed there. It was used only as a holding area until prisoners could be taken to the county seat. Hester preceded Kyle into the bleak building.

The two boys were in separate cells, each one having a metal cot, a lavatory, and a water closet. Kyle pushed a chair to one corner of the room and motioned Hester toward it.

"I'll do the talking," he said and she meekly and silently sat down.

One of the boys was stooped and lanky, with limp brown hair tied back in a ponytail, and looked to be almost eighteen. The other boy, similar in build and appearance, was a few years younger.

Kyle approached the bars. "My name is Kyle Trent," he said. "I'm a lawyer."

"Great, man," the older boy said. "It's about time they sent someone to get us out of this cage. Are you a court-appointed mouthpiece? I had one of those once and he didn't do much."

"I didn't come here to represent you. I live out-of-state and won't be available for your defense but I do want to help you. There are too many boys your age who are headed downhill and I want to encourage you to stop while you can."

"Give me a break, man." The older boy did most of the talking and he was belligerent at first, but during the next half hour, Kyle elicited enough information from them so that Hester had a good idea of what had brought the boys to this place. Her fingers flew rapidly over her notebook.

They were brothers, living with a single mother, and had no idea where their father might be. From appearances, Hester deduced that they were probably biracial. Both were school dropouts and neither had ever held a job.

"You know, of course, that you will have to stand trial for this robbery. But I'm going to try and get some help for you. Since neither of you are eighteen years old, there may be a chance that you can receive probation. But unless you make some effort toward improvement, you'll be back in jail within a few months."

"What kind of help?" the younger boy asked.

"I'll have to explore the possibilities in this area. I know there are state programs that will put recalcitrant teenagers in schools to train them for employment, but I have in mind a camping/outdoor program that would be good for boys like you who have always lived in town."

"That camping thing sounds good to me," the older brother said. "But, man, don't those things cost money?"

"If I provide the money, are you willing to go and try to make something of your lives?"

They both nodded dumbly, looking at Kyle as if he were Santa Claus in person.

"I can't promise you anything yet, but I'll try. And another thing, this outdoor program is operated by a foundation that will introduce you to a Christian way of life. That may be the greatest need you have."

He reached inside the cells and took the boys' hands. "I must hurry away now because I have a pressing commitment, but let's take time for a word of prayer."

The two boys awkwardly bowed their heads, but Hester stared spellbound as Kyle prayed, "Lord, You see before You two of Your Creation who are in need of help. During this time of trouble, will You reveal Yourself to them and give them the assurance that they need never face life's problems alone? And, God, use me as an instrument to bring healing and strength to their lives. Amen."

Still without speaking, Hester followed Kyle out to the sidewalk. As they turned toward the hotel she stated, "This isn't the first time you've done something like this."

"I belong to a board of Christian counselors sponsored by the lawyers' bar association in our area. Most attorneys are devastated by the many youth we see going to prison. Our counselors work with first-time offenders to deter them from the path of crime. We win a few but still lose many that we want to save."

"For what my opinion is worth, I think you did a superb job with those two boys. I was impressed."

He flashed her a smile. "Thanks. It's a switch for me to receive praise from you instead of criticism."

Hester did not answer. She was too busy offering up her own prayer of thanksgiving. *I've just been given a sign.*

twelve

An hour before the train was due on Saturday morning, the railroad tracks were lined with people awaiting their first glimpse of the chapel car. A platform had been built between the tracks and the river for the convenience of the dignitaries, but Mayor Stepp was far too excited to remain seated. He prowled up and down the tracks, shaking hands with everyone, saying over and over, "It's a great day for Afterglow."

A train whistle sounded nearby and the mayor scampered off the tracks. Everyone looked for the engine, but none was to be seen. Hester, however, observed Charlie Benson, slipping a wooden toy whistle into his pocket; she recognized it as one he had made for sale at the factory. He grinned slyly at Hester.

"You're always picking on the mayor," she said with mock severity.

"Someone has to keep him from making a complete fool of himself."

But soon a real whistle sounded far down the valley, heralding the approach of the steam engine, and black smoke billowed into the air as the engine rounded a bend. A shout went up from the onlookers and Mayor Stepp hurried to his seat on the platform.

The big engine roared into town and Hester waved away the cinders falling around her, looking in dismay at the specks of black on her beige jacket. The name, FISHERMAN'S NET, was slashed across the side of the gleaming black car that rolled smoothly behind the Shay engine. Several representatives of the railroad company, which had donated the car, rode in the chapel, as did Iris Hambleton, the descendant of Ivan Hartwell.

Ray and his sister, who had come to Afterglow to represent Mrs. Hartwell, stood on the rear platform, waving to the crowd. When the engine ground to a halt with the screeching of steel on steel and the hiss of escaping steam, ten burly wood hicks stepped close to the platform.

"Move on. Move on," one of them shouted. "We don't want no preachin' and prayin' in this town."

Ray held up his hand in a plea for silence, but the wood hicks drowned out his attempt to speak with catcalls, raucous shouting, and firing of their guns. Three policemen separated themselves from the crowd and brandished weapons to drive the hecklers away.

This bit of drama completed, Mayor Stepp officially accepted the donation of the chapel car and people lined up for tours.

Hester had her notebook handy as she entered the car, which was sixty feet in length and ten feet wide. The sanctuary was long and narrow, with wooden seats on each side of the center aisle. She recognized the portable organ standing beside the pulpit as the one they had seen at Iris Hambleton's. Counting quickly, she estimated that the seating would accommodate 100 worshippers.

Beyond the sanctuary, a small room housed a replica of the missionary's office; a large supply of books lined the walls. The quarters for the missionary and his wife consisted only of a small kitchen and a living room/bedroom combination. Hester marveled at the dedication of those early missionaries who had sacrificed normal living conditions to take the Gospel to isolated communities.

The next morning, the chapel rapidly filled for the dedicatory service, but chairs had been set up on the outside and a microphone had been installed so that everyone could hear.

Deciduous trees on the surrounding mountains had taken on a burnished hue of brown, orange, and deep red during the past week. A smoky haze hovered over the mountain peaks and the sun spread its warm rays around them.

Hester unbuttoned the jacket of the wool suit she had borrowed from Miss Eliza. Since everyone had been asked to wear costumes for this occasion, Kyle and Hester had raided the Byrd attic. She had been able to wear a brown traveling suit that had belonged to Miss Eliza's grandmother. Not knowing how mothworn it was, she had hesitated sending the garment to the cleaners, but the jacket and skirt were too dusty to wear otherwise. The suit had withstood the cleaning, looking almost like new, but it was much too hot for this autumn day.

Kyle had chosen a single-breasted, grayish-brown striped cheviot suit and a stiff hat of the staple open curl style. The hat was made of fur with trimmings and had never been taken from its store wrappings. They had laughed at the price tag of $2.75. Other costumes in the crowd ranged from overalls and flannel shirts worn by the make-believe wood hicks and long full skirts and sunbonnets, to garish buckskin garments that no Indian would have ever worn.

As Hester waited for Ray to begin, she felt a touch of remorse that the celebration was nearly over. Tonight's drama would conclude the centennial observance. Afterglow had been her life for so many intense weeks that she knew she would feel bereft when it was over. Tomorrow, she would start packing to leave for home before the end of the week. Detroit was going to seem dull and lonely after having had hardly a minute of privacy in this small town.

"I'm expecting my answer tomorrow," Kyle whispered as they sat side by side during the instrumental prelude.

"I know."

She still did not know what she would tell him but right now she was more preoccupied with Tommy Byrd, who sat between Miss Eliza and his grandfather in the chapel car. So far she had been able to avoid him and he had not made any effort so speak to her alone, so apparently he recognized her only as a former, mediocre art student.

"To God Be the Glory," resounded around them as the church soloist opened the service. After responsive readings and congregational singing, Ray started his message, using the text from Exodus, " 'And this day shall be unto you for a memorial; and ye shall keep it a feast to the Lord throughout your generations.' "

During the sermon, Ray compared Afterglow's hundred years of history to the journeys of the Hebrews from Egyptian bondage, concluding his brief message with, "The years of our bondage were the times when we lived in a company town and were subjected to exploitation. During that time, Hezekiah Brown was our Pharaoh, but he also became our Moses when he deeded the town of Afterglow to our elected officials and provided a vast legacy for our church.

"We wandered in the wilderness when the timber industry played out, when our furniture factory failed, when the Grand Hotel closed. But folks, we're poised now on the banks of the Jordan and by God's grace, we're going to cross into the Promised Land. Afterglow has had a great past, but we also have a promising future."

Although Hester had practically made up her mind to accept Kyle's proposal, her thoughts took a wayward streak. Ray would certainly make a stable husband and if she married him and stayed in Afterglow, it would be more like answering the Macedonian call she had envisioned. She sighed and Kyle, sensitive to her moods, glanced her way.

It was not difficult to make a choice between "good" and "bad," but what was a woman to do when she had to choose between "good" and "good?" Should she follow her heart?

After the worship service, a town-wide picnic took place. The city fathers had provided a hog and a beef that had been roasting for two days in underground pits. Free beverages had also been supplied from the town's treasury and the women of Afterglow had prepared numerous other foods that were spread on tables along Main Street.

By midafternoon, Hester and Belle left the merrymaking to make preparations for a party they had planned for the cast after the final presentation. They had reserved an empty room at the hotel and they met there to prepare some snacks before show time.

"I am excited about Afterglow's future," Belle chatted as they spread sandwiches with meat filling. "Clint says he has reliable information that the state will buy this hotel for their headquarters."

"So Mayor Stepp said. It's such a lovely building and I'm pleased that it won't deteriorate anymore."

"And the train excursions to Brown's camp will start next summer. I hope you'll come back to ride one of them."

"I would enjoy riding up that mountain on a train rather than Ray's four-wheeler. I'll never forget how terrified I was the first time we did that." She shuddered. "In spite of his faults, we'll have to admit that Mayor Stepp is a man with vision. I'm eager to see how he'll react to the surprise we have for him."

"Oh, he'll be excited because he knows that Afterglow's future is secure. But what about yours, Hester? I'm not exactly blind. Is it going to be Kyle or Ray?"

"Definitely not Ray; I've told him so. I'm not cut out for small-town living. I've not given Kyle an answer, so it may not be him, either."

"We had hoped it would be Ray so we could keep you here in Afterglow, but you have our best wishes, whatever you decide."

❧

For the final performance, the ballroom was packed. People stood around the walls, willing to pay for standing room in order to see the drama. Mayor Stepp had already asked Hester if she would return next year and direct the drama for a few weeks during the summertime, but Hester declined.

"You won't need me. You have the script and someone else can take over."

After the final curtain call, Ray came onstage.

"To conclude our centennial observation, we want to recognize and give thanks to the person who has done the most to make this celebration a reality. Mayor Stepp, will you come forward?"

The mayor rose from his chair slowly, not with his usual vibrancy, and that uncharacteristic action convinced Hester of his surprise. When he stepped onstage, Ray continued, "Mayor Stepp, tonight we are presenting you with this plaque to recognize your belief in the future of Afterglow and for your promotion of this celebration. One hundred years ago, Hezekiah Brown gave birth to this town, but your efforts have given us a new lease on life and a hope for another century of achievement. Therefore, we award you the Hezekiah Brown Award as Afterglow's most outstanding citizen."

Ray shook the mayor's hand and gave him the plaque. The audience rose as one person and greeted the presentation with thunderous applause. Mayor Stepp clutched the plaque, and when the people quieted, Ray motioned for the mayor to speak. Tears streamed down his face and he opened his lips several times, but no words came. With a wave to the audience, he tottered off the stage. For once, the mayor was speechless!

Hester sank wearily into a chair, but she still had the cast's party to oversee so she could not collapse yet. She had already made up her mind that she was taking a vacation before she returned to her job. She stirred from the chair and made an effort to be entertaining, but during the two hours the party lasted, she looked forward to some rest.

Rest, though, was not to be hers for several more hours, for when she returned to her small house, Tommy Byrd was waiting on the steps. She stopped abruptly when she saw him; she was too surprised to speak, but thankful she had parted from Kyle at the front of the main house.

"I'm leaving in the morning and I thought we should have a talk before I go," he said. "You can't keep avoiding me. May I come in?"

Hester nodded and with trembling fingers, she opened the door. She took her coat and purse into the bedroom, and when she returned, Tommy was observing *Winter Serenity*.

"I always wondered why that painting resembled Afterglow."

"And now you know," he said. "But just how much else do you know?"

She went into the bedroom again to collect the letter she had received in Detroit and the pack of letters she had found in the desk. She handed those to him and motioned him toward a chair.

"That's all the information I have. You read them while I make some tea."

She took her time preparing the beverage and when she returned with the tray, he laid the letters aside. A light rain had started and the incessant drip on the front step set Hester's nerves atingle.

"So you know that I'm your father?"

"Yes. I learned it from that packet of letters in the old desk. But I wasn't sure you knew my identity."

"I've been a regular subscriber to your Detroit newspaper since you were born, Hester. I've kept up with you that way."

"So even when I was a student in your art class, you knew I was your daughter?"

"Yes."

"But why did you give me away?" Hester said, the pain of rejection evident in her voice.

"At the time Anna approached me about a divorce, I wasn't sure I would recover from my injury, and even if I did, I didn't know when I'd find a job. There wasn't much I could do with a baby, nor could I have paid child support at that time. It was obvious that Anna had made a mistake to marry me. I checked out John Lawson and he seemed an honorable man. So I had to let you go. I didn't suppose you would ever know, but I deduced that you did by the way you acted a few days ago when you saw me."

"I probably wouldn't have known if that old letter hadn't arrived. You've never married again?"

"No. I loved Anna and there was no one to take her place."

"John Lawson was a good father and I loved him, so no harm came to me. But I do feel hurt that I wasn't told by someone. At my age it was shattering for me to suspect that my birth was somewhat clouded."

"Except for a freak accident by the postal department, you would never have known. I probably shouldn't have said anything to you since it was obvious you didn't want to discuss it, but the truth is, Hester, I've done without my daughter for thirty years. I would never have interfered as long as your other parents lived. But now that they're gone, I'd like for us to be friends, even if we can't develop a father/daughter relationship."

"I would like that. We had good rapport during that university class, so I suppose that was mutual blood drawing us together. And you're certainly the type of person anyone would be proud to own as a father."

"I'm proud of you, too."

"Are we going to tell the people in Afterglow?"

"They've probably had all the surprises they can take right now. Perhaps we can have Clint publish it in the newspaper at a later time."

"The past six months have been frustrating and it seems I've been in the midst of every controversy."

His smile reminded Hester of Miss Eliza. "I'm going on a photo safari to Kenya around the first of December. If you're returning to Detroit, I can contact you there when I return."

Hester brought a notepad from the desk. "I'll give you my address and telephone number. I'll look forward to hearing from you." He folded the paper and tucked it into his pocket.

"I'm intending to buy this desk and take it back to Detroit with me. Not only do I like its utility, but it has a sentimental value to me, too, since it revealed the secret of my past. I suppose it's really your desk. Do you mind?"

He shook his head and she explained how Charlie Benson had found the letters in the top, and Tommy smiled.

"I've wondered for years what happened to those letters and feared the wrong person would find them. I suppose you were the right one to discover them."

"What's your home address? Miss Eliza didn't seem to know."

"I didn't want anyone to know. I have an apartment in Manhattan and I'm there more than anyplace else, but I have so many appointments in and out of the country that I'm seldom at home." He handed her a calling card with his address and telephone number. "I won't be of much bother to you."

"I truly want to keep in touch for I've felt very alone since my mother died."

"I'm lonely, too, and I want to share your life. I'm sure we'll soon develop a filial relationship."

ð

That night, Hester went to bed more relaxed and at peace than she had been for over a year. She looked forward to knowing Tommy Byrd. She had admired his excellent artwork for years, but now she would know him as a father. She had missed John Lawson and she felt fortunate to have someone to take his place. She repeated slowly the words on the sampler in the kitchen, "In all thy ways acknowledge Him and He shall direct thy paths." God did have a purpose in directing her to Afterglow.

Kyle's knock came before she finished her breakfast. *Have I ever eaten a meal here that hasn't been interrupted?*

She opened the door and he followed her into the kitchen. "I'm packed, ready to shake the dust of Afterglow from my feet. What's your answer?" he asked.

Although he spoke in his usual jaunty fashion, Hester detected a worried look in his eyes. He obviously feared she might reject him.

"Sit down, Kyle. If you've already eaten Miss Eliza's breakfast, you aren't hungry, but pour yourself some tea."

When he sat across from her, a cup in his hand, she said, "I think it's yes."

His eyes brightened and she lifted her hand. "But we've been thrown together under such unusual circumstances all summer that I feel we should take a few more months to make our final decision. We're dealing with a lifetime, nothing to take lightly. I'm sure I love you, but I don't know if we will be compatible."

Seriously, he said, "I realize that and I'm willing to take some more time. Why don't we start a normal courtship. . . telephone calls and visits when we have time? It isn't far from Detroit to Harrisburg on interstates and we could visit at least once a month."

"That's what I have in mind. We've both lived alone more than most couples who marry. We're independent in many ways. It will take some adjustment."

"You don't have a family to consider, but you should meet mine. Perhaps you could come to Harrisburg for Christmas."

Deciding to wait a while before telling him about Tommy Byrd, she said, "I don't see any reason why I can't, and this seems the best way. Hasty marriages don't always work." She had ample reason to know that from the fiasco of her parents' union.

They exchanged addresses and telephone numbers and Kyle stood to leave. "Can't we at least seal our sort-of engagement with a kiss?"

Willingly, Hester went into Kyle's arms. From force of habit, she glanced to be sure the window shades were open, but then she smiled when his lips hovered over hers. These months in Afterglow had taught her the truth of Proverbs 22:1: "A good name is rather to be chosen than great riches."

A Letter To Our Readers

Dear Reader:

In order that we might better contribute to your reading enjoyment, we would appreciate your taking a few minutes to respond to the following questions. When completed, please return to the following:

Rebecca Germany, Managing Editor
Heartsong Presents
P.O. Box 719
Uhrichsville, Ohio 44683

1. Did you enjoy reading *Afterglow*?
   ❑ Very much. I would like to see more books
      by this author!
   ❑ Moderately
      I would have enjoyed it more if _____
      _____

2. Are you a member of **Heartsong Presents**? ❑Yes ❑No
   If no, where did you purchase this book?_____
   _____

3. What influenced your decision to purchase this
   book? (Check those that apply.)

   ❑ Cover   ❑ Back cover copy

   ❑ Title   ❑ Friends

   ❑ Publicity   ❑ Other_____

4. How would you rate, on a scale from 1 (poor) to 5
   (superior), the cover design?_____

5. On a scale from 1 (poor) to 10 (superior), please rate the following elements.

      ___Heroine   ___Plot

      ___Hero   ___Inspirational theme

      ___Setting   ___Secondary characters

6. What settings would you like to see covered in **Heartsong Presents** books?_____

_____

_____

7. What are some inspirational themes you would like to see treated in future books?_____

_____

_____

8. Would you be interested in reading other **Heartsong Presents** titles?   ❑ Yes   ❑ No

9. Please check your age range:
   ❑ Under 18   ❑ 18-24   ❑ 25-34
   ❑ 35-45   ❑ 46-55   ❑ Over 55

10. How many hours per week do you read? _____

Name _____

Occupation _____

Address _____

City_____ State_____ Zip _____

·········· Presents ··········

Hearts♥ng Presents
Love Stories Are Rated G!

That's for godly, gratifying, and of course, great! If you love a thrilling love story, but don't appreciate the sordidness of some popular paperback romances, **Heartsong Presents** is for you. In fact, **Heartsong Presents** is the *only inspirational romance book club*, the only one featuring love stories where Christian faith is the primary ingredient in a marriage relationship.

Sign up today to receive your first set of four, never before published Christian romances. Send no money now; you will receive a bill with the first shipment. You may cancel at any time without obligation, and if you aren't completely satisfied with any selection, you may return the books for an immediate refund!

Imagine. . .four new romances every four weeks—two historical, two contemporary—with men and women like you who long to meet the one God has chosen as the love of their lives. . .all for the low price of $9.97 postpaid.

To join, simply complete the coupon below and mail to the address provided. **Heartsong Presents** romances are rated G for another reason: They'll arrive *Godspeed!*